A TALE OF GOLD

ALSO BY THELMA HATCH WYSS

Bear Dancer: The Story of a Ute Girl

MARGARET K. MCELDERRY BOOKS

A TALE OF
GOLD

THELMA HATCH WYSS

MARGARET K. MCELDERRY BOOKS
NEW YORK   LONDON   TORONTO   SYDNEY

FOR MICHAEL PORTER

Margaret K. McElderry Books
An imprint of Simon & Schuster Children's Publishing Division
1230 Avenue of the Americas, New York, New York 10020
Book design by Krista Vossen
The text for this book is set in Apollo.
Manufactured in the United States of America
2 4 6 8 10 9 7 5 3 1
Library of Congress Cataloging-in-Publication Data
Wyss, Thelma Hatch.
A tale of gold / Thelma Hatch Wyss.—1st ed.
p. cm.
Summary: Orphaned, fourteen-year-old James decides to join the "stampeders" heading to the Yukon gold rush, and along the way joins up with two unusual partners who all find a common bond of wanting to strike it rich.
ISBN-13: 978-1-4169-4212-2 (hardcover)
ISBN-10: 1-4169-4212-2 (hardcover)
[1. Friendship—Fiction. 2. Orphans—Fiction. 3. Gold mines and mining—Yukon Territory—Klondike River Valley—Fiction. 4. Klondike River Valley (Yukon)—History—19th century—Fiction. 5. Yukon Territory—History—19th century—Fiction.] I. Title.
PZ7.W998Tal 2007
[Fic]—dc22
2006037545

"All my life," he said, "I have searched for the treasure. I have sought it in the high places, and in the narrow—and yet have not found it.

"Instead, at the end of every trail, I have found you awaiting me. And now you have become familiar to me, though I cannot say I know you well.

"Who are you?"

And the stranger answered:

"Thyself."

—FROM AN OLD TALE

Contents

I SEEK MY FORTUNE

I remember the day I saw the grizzled old man dragging his suitcases down the gangplank of the *Excelsior*, just docked in the San Francisco harbor. It was the fifteenth of July, 1897.

I was fourteen years old that summer, the youngest hack driver on the waterfront, transporting with my rented horse and wagon anything the steamers discharged. But that July morning when the *Excelsior* spewed out her strange-looking passengers, even the oldest hack driver, Old Andy, held his horse in rein.

Behind the old grizzled man a cluster of men and women staggered down the gangplank, dragging suitcases and boxes. They all had the same fearful look, as if they had experienced something horrible together.

Cannibals, I thought. And so must have Rexy, my horse, for her ears shot forward and she whinnied piteously.

The old man looked up in our direction, squinting, as if the sun were rising right there on the cobble-stones of the Embarcadero.

"Hack," he called.

My pa had told me time and again: "James Erickson, son, beggars can't be choosers."

He may have told Rexy, too, for she trotted right over to the gangplank without my lifting the reins. Rexy was one smart horse. She knew I'd give any-one a ride for twenty-five cents—even a cannibal.

Closer up, the old man looked even more forbid-ding. Under a grimy, wide-brimmed hat his gray hair stuck out like wire, and his whiskers were matted around his scarred face. His eyes glowed with an unnatural light—like a man slightly mad.

He grinned, and I saw he was toothless. "Just in from the Klondike," he slurred. "Can you give me a hand with my suitcases?"

I jumped down from my wagon. The old man had not the strength to lift two suitcases.

Nor had I. It took both of us grappling together to lift each suitcase into the wagon. I didn't like it. I didn't like hauling dead bones around.

After the old man was satisfied that his suitcases were secure in the back, he climbed up on the seat next to me.

"Quick, lad," he whispered. "To Selby's. Selby's in North Beach."

I knew Selby's. Selby's Smelting Works on Montgomery Street. Then suddenly, I also knew the contents of those two suitcases. Not bones—just solid gold.

At Selby's I helped the old man drag his suitcases inside, pulling with the frayed ropes.

"Here," he said. He reached into a leather pouch hanging from his belt and handed me a gold piece the size of a hen's egg. "Wait for me outside."

I stared in disbelief. "I-I've no change for that, sir," I stammered.

"No matter," the man said with a grin.

I then suspected he was a bank robber, and I waited uneasily in my wagon.

When the old man returned, he climbed up beside me. "Now to the Palace," he roared.

I didn't question him. I took him to the Palace Hotel—all the way back across town to the end of Montgomery Street, trotting Rexy through the arched driveway right alongside the fountains of the marble-paved Grand Court.

He didn't ask me to, but I waited. I thought that after he was tossed out of the most opulent hotel in the city, I could take him home with me to Mrs. Maxwell's—not saying he was a bank robber, of course. And Mrs. Maxwell, who took in almost anyone, because of hard times, would—if he washed in the Bay first—take him in.

As I waited, I pulled my cap down over my eyes so I could bask in the elegance of the Grand Court without staring. Although I had never been inside the magnificent hotel, I knew its interior matched the grandeur of the courtyard. I knew it had eight hundred rooms with eight hundred noiseless water closets. Everyone in the city knew that.

After waiting half an hour, I thought perhaps he had been thrown out the back door. I was just telling Rexy to quit staring and start moving, when I heard a sound like falling pebbles. I looked up—seven floors up—and there in a window I saw the old man. He was waving his ragged arms and tossing gold nuggets like confetti to the courtyard below. He was shouting a crazy song:

As I walk along the Bois Boo-long
With an independent air,
You can hear the girls declare,
"He must be a millionaire."

Rexy and I had no more business that afternoon, so at sunset, as the fog began to roll in, we headed back to Almo's Livery on Front Street. I fed and watered Rexy, as I was required to do each night, and gave her a rubdown, which was not required.

Rexy was a beauty—all black with one narrow strip of white down the center of her face. On her neck was a scar that I often wondered about, and I tried to make it up to her with the rubdowns. I think she understood.

That night I lingered longer than usual because I wanted to tell Almo about the gold nugget burning in my pocket. He was one of the few people I talked to, I suppose because he and Pa used to talk a lot.

I was surprised he didn't call out as soon as I walked in, "What's that burning a hole in your pocket, James?"

But tonight he was talking to Old Andy. So I just waved and started home. Maybe I'd tell Mrs. Maxwell.

Home was south of Market, in a faded green boarding house clinging to the side of Rincon Hill.

It was the only green house in a row of pink and orange ones, also faded. Except for the colors, they all looked alike: steps leading up to a small arched porch, a bay window on the first floor, a bay window on the second, and a dormer window in the attic, all surrounded with elaborate woodwork, which made me think that elves had lived there once. Because the house was the only green one, it was easy to find in the fog.

My room was the one with the dormer window. On a clear day I could see everything—the blue sky and the blue San Francisco Bay with the white-and-orange ferryboats crossing back and forth to Oakland. And the Berkeley Hills in the distance.

Pa and I had stopped here a year earlier because the train had. We looked around and found Mrs. Maxwell's boardinghouse, and then we found Almo's Livery, and we became hack drivers.

Whenever luck ran out for Pa, he just walked to the nearest railroad depot, boarded a train, and got off at a place he liked the looks of.

The first place I remember was Omaha, Nebraska. I was five. After my mother died, my pa took my hand and we climbed aboard a Union Pacific train. The next day we got off at Rock Springs, Wyoming, because Pa liked the looks of it when the train slowed down.

We became ranch hands. We stayed there until hard times came and the ranchers could not pay their hired help. So we boarded a train again and got off at San Francisco, where we became hack drivers.

We liked it at Mrs. Maxwell's, even though the boarders were faded like the house and the talk at the table was always the same—President McKinley and the depression.

Including Pa and me, there were eight boarders at Mrs. Maxwell's. Two of them were elderly sisters who never smiled because of the depression—and it had been going on for four years.

Pa told funny stories about himself, and most people laughed and asked for more. One night at supper, he told about having his tooth pulled on the ranch in Rock Springs, and Mrs. Maxwell laughed so hard she could not dish up the dessert. The story went like this:

Pa had suffered from a toothache for a long time. So when a traveling dentist came around, Pa asked him to pull it.

Pa sat down on a bench outside the bunkhouse and the dentist went to work. He pulled and pulled at that tooth. When it finally came out, Pa's head bounced back against the bunkhouse and he was knocked out cold. When he came to, he looked up at the startled dentist.

"Next time," Pa said, "apply the anesthetic first!"

The two sisters never cracked a smile. We chuckled a good deal over them, however, upstairs in our room.

I was a lot like Pa, but not in telling funny stories. In my first fourteen years nothing funny had happened to me, at least nothing I thought was funny.

In most other ways we were alike: two lanky, bowlegged, blue-eyed cowboys, not long off the boat from Norway, with the Viking blood of our ancestors roaring through our veins. Looking for something to conquer.

At least, that's what Pa said.

Pa died in that boardinghouse, from pneumonia. He was only sick for three days and he never saw a doctor. On the third day Mrs. Maxwell sent up some ginger tea and a hot-water bottle. He told me to go to work. When I came home that night, he was gone.

I knew he did not want to leave me. And he had not expected to when he'd told me to go to work that morning. It just happened.

I still talked to Pa in the evenings as I walked home to Mrs. Maxwell's in the fog, telling him about my day and asking his advice about things. But each evening it became more painfully clear that he could not answer.

I walked home that summer evening in July with the fog licking my heels, talking to my pa about a golden nugget in my pocket. Not asking—just talking.

The next morning I found that my world, like the old man at the Palace Hotel, had gone completely mad.

At first, when I heard all the commotion downstairs, I thought the house was on fire. I grabbed my pants and pulled them on going down the stairs.

All the boarders were gathered around the kitchen table, reading the morning newspaper out loud. The two sisters were smiling.

"James, James," they both shouted, waving the newspaper. "The depression is over. The depression is over!"

The message was spread across the front page of the *Chronicle*: GOLD! GOLD! GOLD! DEPRESSION OVER!

"A ship of gold came in," Mrs. Maxwell shouted above the clamor. "A ship of gold from up North in the Yukon Territory. On the Klondike!"

"Folks just picked it up and put it in their suitcases," old Mrs. Howard said. "It says so right here." She pointed. "Millionaires overnight—Tom Lippy, Hestwood, Joe Ladue, Louis Rhodes—"

"Bet those suitcases were heavy," Mr. Adamson shouted.

"Bet they didn't care," Mr. Call said, grinning.

Mr. McPhee grabbed Mrs. Howard and they danced around the table. Mrs. Howard held his collar with one hand and her wig with the other.

"We'll have to build another Nob Hill," Mr. Adamson shrieked in my ear.

I sat down at the table in dizzy bewilderment. "I saw them," I said. "Dragging their suitcases bulging with gold. I gave one a ride—"

No one was listening to me. So I ate my eggs and

toast, smiling to myself. That crazy old miner had started a gold stampede and ended the depression overnight.

"You're late, kid," Almo yelled, although eight o'clock was the time I always arrived at the livery. "Waterfront's hopping like the Easter bunny. Everybody's going North. Gold up there! Everybody's crowding on steamers. Everybody's going crazy, buying boots and shovels and dehydrated eggs and wanting it hauled from one place to another—"

Almo took a quick breath. "Yelling for hacks to haul their bacon and beans and boots. Everybody's crazy!"

I could see that, all right. And the madness continued all summer. From all over the country, men rushed to San Francisco. They slept on doorsteps and in liveries and washed at fire hydrants.

It was said, though I did not see it with my own eyes, that dentists left their patients sitting in chairs, railroad conductors left their passengers stranded, preachers left their congregations, and barbers left their shops with customers half-shaven.

I saw them all at the waterfront, however, milling around in their new high-top boots and wide-brimmed hats, waiting to crowd aboard the next ship headed North. It was madness. It was called "gold fever."

I didn't think of going North myself. I guess I didn't have time to think about it. Rexy nearly trotted her legs off for me that summer—up and down those cobblestone hills, racing the noisy cable cars along Powell Street. Rexy and I did not need to go North for gold. We would be rich in no time staying at home.

Anyone could tell Rexy was one smart horse. And every day someone would offer to buy her.

"Give you thirty dollars for the horse."

"She's not for sale," I said, over and over again.

Early in September, Rexy disappeared. I arrived at the livery that morning at eight o'clock as usual and saw her empty stall. I whistled for her, but there was no answer.

"Where's Rexy?" I called to Almo out in back.

Almo shuffled to the doorway, his massive form blocking out the morning light. "You tell me," he said.

"What do you mean?" I asked. "She was in her stall last night when I left. What happened? Where is she?"

Almo still leaned in the doorway, chewing a straw. "That'll be fifty dollars, kid, or I'll call the law."

I was dumbfounded. "Almo, someone has stolen

her. You know I wouldn't. You know me. You knew my pa—"

Almo snarled. "No horse, no job."

"Almo—you're joking. Let me rent another horse until I find her."

He shook his head.

"I didn't steal her, Almo. And I didn't sell her," I said firmly. "And you know that. But I will look for her—until I find her."

"No horse, no job," Almo said again.

I searched for Rexy for a week. I was so tired each evening I could hardly drag my feet home.

One evening going home, I saw Mrs. Maxwell standing in the doorway shaking her head. She had rented my attic room to one of *them*.

This time I heard Pa talking loud and clear. "James Erickson, son," he said. "Time to move on."

I stuffed all my belongings—and Pa's meager savings—into a knapsack and took off down Market Street, wondering how I had mistaken duty for kindness. I resolved then I would not make the mistake again.

I turned, waved good-bye to the faded green house floating in the fog, and then hastened toward the harbor.

To an orphan, it does not matter if he is three

blocks from the place he lives or three thousand miles. Therefore, it was not so unusual that at the age of fourteen I set out alone for the Far North, with a gold nugget in my pocket, to seek my fortune.

· CHAPTER 2 ·

NORTH ON THE *GUARDIAN*

One hundred thousand stampeders set out for the Klondike goldfields that year, and it seemed to me that they were all crowded on the decks of the *Guardian*.

The *Guardian* was on her way to the boneyard when the stampede began. She was turned around, lined up in the docks with other unseaworthy vessels, and called a steamship.

I did not complain. I was lucky to be on board.

Wandering around the waterfront, I had happened to see a man doubled over, obviously in great pain. His partner was guiding him toward a hack and, at the same time, was auctioning his steamship ticket.

I pushed in close and shouted, "Two hundred cash."

"Sold!" The partner handed me a green ticket:

1ST CLASS FARE—SAN FRANCISCO TO SKAGWAY, ALASKA—$100.

I clutched the ticket in my hand and hurried to the steamer. "Thanks, Pa," I whispered. "It was from your savings."

The *Guardian* had accommodations for one hundred passengers. But there were on her decks five hundred men, along with horses, mules, dogs, and sheep. In my cabin were twelve men and three berths. All the cabins were oversold.

The purser screamed that anyone who did not like it could get off at the first coal stop—or immediately, and two more men would take his place.

"Throw them all overboard," a voice bellowed from the pilothouse.

"Who's the big mouth up there?" a burly man asked, rolling up his sleeves.

"It's the ship's captain," the purser yelled, pushing him back.

The crowd was stunned into silence. Then someone shouted, "How's the captain steering this wreck if he's drunk already?"

The purser did not answer.

I pushed through the crowd to the foredeck, where the horses were quartered in crude stalls. Bales of hay were piled up to the pilothouse windows. I supposed that looking down into a horse corral was reason enough for the captain to drink.

After one sleepless night in the crowded cabin, our group organized. The biggest man, a policeman from Colorado, wrote out a time schedule with bylaws and nailed it to the cabin door.

Each of us would have a berth in the cabin for six hours a day. Only personal bags were to be left in the cabin—grubstakes and dogs were to be left in the hall or up on deck. Our schedule would rotate every four days. There were to be no complaints.

The policeman drew names from a derby hat for cabinmates. I ended up with Snorin' Sam and Mr. Con Man. The con man may have snored also, but I never found that out. He spent all his time in the cabin going through the bags.

He was as smooth as his black oiled hair. During our first shift he confessed that he was afraid to sleep in the top bunk because of his fear of heights. Once as a child he had fallen from the roof of his house, he said.

It didn't matter to me. I slept in the top bunk in my clothes with my money stashed in the bottom of my stockings and the gold nugget deep in my pocket. Using my knapsack as a pillow, I lay on my stomach with one arm over my eyes.

Mr. Con Man had the bottom bunk. He was always quiet until Sam in the middle bunk began snoring. Then he would call up to me.

"Sleeps like a log, don't he?"

I never answered.

"You a light sleeper, kid?"

In a few minutes he would stand up and look at me with his dark beady eyes.

"Asleep, kid?" he would ask. Then he would go through the bags.

I thought of saying something to the policeman, but I kept quiet. I was trying out some of Pa's advice. "James Erickson, son," he had said, "be like the Sphinx. Look wise, but don't say too much."

The schedule worked fine for temporary. And we all knew it would be just a few weeks until we were rich. Then never again would we be required to adjust to life's inconveniences.

Each day after our allotted time in the cabin, we hurried upstairs and stood in two lines, one for the dining room and one for the water closets. The men were always in a rush, which seemed a little strange because there were not many places to rush to—just those two. But they rushed from line to line, just the same.

The thing I did not like about the schedule was that it placed me in Mr. Con Man's company so much. I kept our conversations short.

"You don't seem to have a grubstake, son," he said, sidling up to me in the dining room line.

"Not yet." I concentrated on the beef carcasses hanging in a line next to us. I counted the ribs.

"Don't seem to have a partner, either, son."

"Not yet. And the name's Erickson."

"Just call me Dad," he said smoothly.

When not in lines, the men sprawled on top of their grubstakes, playing solitaire. Hating each other. Scheming how to get off the ship faster and how to pick up gold faster than everyone else.

After the first week, they became so bored that they began talking and playing cards together, and soon several partnerships were formed. I hoped that someone would get bored enough to want to hitch up with a kid. But no one did.

Mostly I sat on the hay bales, talking to the horses and wishing I could find Rexy on that ship. Sometimes from the hay bales I talked to Captain Hillis, who liked conversation as much as the bottle.

We sailed north up the coastlines of California, Oregon, and Washington, our small steamer rocking in the rough waters. When we reached Vancouver Island, we sailed around its southern tip to Victoria and from there entered the sheltered waters of the Inside Passage.

"There's an island portside," I told Captain Hillis one day when the fog was heavy. We were somewhere in the Inside Passage, surrounded by tall pine trees and low clouds.

"Tarnation! Didn't see it," he exclaimed. He blew the ship's whistle as if to tell the island to move over. Later he told me that he blew the whistle to judge by its echo how close the ship was to the shore.

But wherever I was on that ship, Mr. Con Man was never far away.

"You say you're meeting your partner in Skagway, son?"

"That's the plan."

"You intending to buy your supplies when you get there?"

"That's the plan."

One day there was a little excitement that broke the routine. I was on the foredeck talking to the horses when a gang of red-faced men roared up to the pilothouse, threatening to kill the captain.

"Our berths," they snarled, "are right below here." They pointed to the horse stalls. "Just below the horses, to be exact."

"So?" Captain Hillis sneered.

"So there are cracks in the deck," one man yelled. "Wide cracks. And what the horses do, drips through on us." He paused for emphasis. "And it ain't rain!"

Captain Hillis looked shocked. He moved toward the door, nodding and smiling, waving the men out ahead of him. As the men moved back from the door, he quickly slammed it shut and locked it.

"Go tell the horses," he yelled through a window.

I laughed on the foredeck until my sides hurt. I could laugh, of course, because my cabin was in the stern.

The scenery was beautiful. Two thousand miles of lush evergreeen forests, deep blue fjords, snow-capped mountains, lacy waterfalls, and silver glaciers drifting silently out to sea.

It was hardly noticed at all, except for a few icebergs that nearly hit us off Prince Rupert. And the totem poles near Ketchikan almost scared the wits out of us. When those tall painted faces with beaks and wings loomed through the fog, I saw men shudder with fright.

But all that scenery might just as well have been painted on a picture postcard for all the stampeders cared. They complained when the ship made coal stops, saying the captain was trying to delay them. That's how bad they had the gold fever.

Except for the excitement over the horses, and the scare of the icebergs and totem poles, those two weeks dragged by much the same until the dance-hall girls got on at Juneau, toward the end of our journey.

When the steamer pulled up to the towering mountain of Juneau, the men yelled, "If one more person gets on this old tub, we'll sink for sure!"

But when they saw the four young ladies stepping up the gangplank, they began cheering. That pleased the ladies, and they lifted their long skirts and kicked a cancan right there on the gangplank. Hidden under those long skirts were colored ruffles and black lace stockings with silver-spangled garters.

A skinny boy also came aboard, although he was hardly noticed because of the dancing girls. When he was standing alone, I asked if he would like to go see the horses. He must have been seasick, because he turned and fled.

The following day, as Captain Hillis piloted the steamer up the narrowing Lynn Canal, he said to me, "Do you know about Skagway, James?"

All I knew about Skagway was that it was the outfitting place at the foot of the Coast Mountains that we had to cross to reach the Klondike goldfields.

"It's the windiest place on earth," the captain said. "Windy. Cold. Ugly. All the buildings are covered with black tar paper, flapping day and night, to keep out the north wind."

He pulled a face as if he were seasick.

"Winds don't bother me," I said. I was anxious to get there.

"There's something in Skagway far worse than the wind," the captain said.

"Oh?" I waited impatiently.

Captain Hillis did not say more. He just shook his head.

At Skagway, the *Guardian* was met by a parade of cowboys, who rode their horses down the long wooden wharf, whooping and hollering. A minister pranced his dapple-gray horse right up the gangplank and shouted, "Welcome to Skagway!"

I ducked past the welcoming committee and hurried down the long wharf built out over the tidal flats, where steamers and scows had dropped their freight and animals.

Dogs were barking. Horses were rearing and snorting. Men were cussing and dragging their goods through the mud, trying to beat the tide to the high-water line. It was a mad scene.

Up above, the scenery was another picture postcard—mountains, covered in dark cotton-wood and spruce trees, rising thousands of feet above the beach, their lonely peaks somewhere up there above the clouds. Green mountains, glacial green waterfalls—

But no one was looking up. And I didn't either, for long.

I moved with the crowd, around tents and camp-fires to the main street of town, called Broadway. The loudest music I had ever heard came surging from that makeshift tar-paper street. Loud enough to wake the dead, Pa would say.

On the boardwalk a gypsy organ-grinder was cranking out a tune and singing:

When you hear dem-a bells go ding ling ling,
All join 'round, and sweetly you must sing,
And when the verse am through,
In the chorus all join in,
There'll be a hot time in the old town tonight!

His little monkey jumped up onto his shoulder to avoid being trampled and held out a tin cup hopefully.

Suddenly a bullet whizzed overhead. It pierced the cup and the wall behind. The frightened monkey dropped the cup and covered his eyes.

The crowd laughed hideously, then sang along with the organ-grinder:

And when the verse am through,
In the chorus all join in,
There'll be a hot time in the old town tonight!

I could tell Skagway was a good place to get out of. And I'd be getting out—as soon as I looked around.

• CHAPTER 3 •

SOMETHING IN SKAGWAY

I was looking around for Rexy. So I parted company with the Broadway crowd and made my way to a side street with fewer people and less noise.

Tents and shacks were set up for business. Hanging from one tent was an old pair of trousers with MEALS scrawled across the seat. I went inside and had a stack of sourdough pancakes.

I inquired about horses.

The cook bellowed, "For eating or for packing?"

That brought him a big round of laughter. My face turned red.

"I'll tell you the truth, *cheechako*," the cook said, loud enough for everyone to hear. "Every tent that says 'Meals' has them for eating, and all the others are on the White Pass."

I hurried out of there and wandered around the streets.

Although Captain Hillis had suggested I stay at

Mrs. Pullen's boardinghouse, I ignored his advice. I went into the first tent I saw advertising cots for fifty cents.

Just as I was dozing off, I saw a strange sight, although nothing seemed completely abnormal anymore. About a dozen men, scattered throughout the tent, rose from their cots and began fleecing the other sleeping men. They emptied leather pokes and pockets. They pulled off boots—those that would come off—and took the paper money hidden there. And also the boots.

All the while the weary prospectors slept on in oblivion, snoring and wheezing.

In a panic, but quietly, I removed my shoes and the contents of my pockets. I shoved everything into my knapsack and rolled over on top of it, hoping I looked like I had already been fleeced.

And although I intended to keep one eye open all night, I soon fell asleep.

The first thing I did the next morning was to find Pullen's Boardinghouse down on the waterfront. I must have looked rather seedy, because when Mrs. Pullen answered the door, she frowned. After I told her that Captain Hillis had told me to come, she smiled.

"Just surface dirt, then," she said. "Come on in. Breakfast is in thirty minutes."

I might have guessed. The four dance-hall girls

from Juneau were there, and the skinny boy. Five stampeders were there also.

No one said much because Mrs. Pullen did the talking, as well as the cooking. She carried on a monologue as she went in and out of the dining room.

"Just read a book, young man," she said, "for about two weeks while it snows. Or chop wood for me. After two weeks of snow and a good freeze, both passes will be open. And you can go scrambling after your gold and not get killed by avalanches.

"When the Tlingit Indians stay out of the passes, I tell my boarders to stay out of the passes. That way we'll all get rich and still stay alive."

The two passes Mrs. Pullen referred to were the Chilkoot Pass and the White Pass. Both had been secret Indian trails over the Coast Mountains. Until the gold stampede.

"Now," Mrs. Pullen continued as she came into the dining room with a platter of pancakes, "I don't suppose any of you brought your own horses. Stampeders with pack animals go White Pass until the animals drop dead. It's already called 'Dead Horse Trail.' Men packing their own supplies— and Indian packers—go Chilkoot. I'd suggest, for the girls anyway, to go Chilkoot."

The dance-hall girls called themselves the "Flower

Girls," and their names were Pansy, Violet, Petunia, and Daisy. They were on their way to the Klondike to sing and dance for the prospectors.

"Now, you know," Mrs. Pullen said, "that you cannot enter Canada without a year's supply of food, almost a ton of goods. The North West Mounted Police just won't let you. First thing you know, they'll be at the top of each pass with machine guns lined up on the snowdrifts. No one slips past a Mountie. Not even Soapy Smith's con men."

"Con men?" Daisy asked.

"Con men are all over Skagway and both trails, and Soapy Smith is their leader. He started out selling soap. Now it's organized crime. But they can't get past the Mounties. You girls just stick together and keep your eyes open. And you men find yourselves an honest partner—one sleeps while the other watches—and you'll make it."

I knew what she was talking about there.

"Now eat," she continued, "and you girls quit worrying about your little waists. Then go read your dime novels."

I looked up quickly. In the boardinghouse on Rincon Hill no one read dime novels. No one even said the words.

I glanced at the Flower Girls, who did not seem surprised at all. I supposed, like dime novels, they too were frowned upon by proper society.

After breakfast that mollycoddled boy went straight to the parlor and read a dime novel. I chopped wood for Mrs. Pullen for an hour. Then I went inside and said to him, "Want to go looking for horses with me?"

He looked up over that book as if he were seasick again. "No thanks," he said. "I'm reading."

I did not think Soapy Smith and his con men would come bothering Mrs. Pullen, so I left most of my money in my knapsack under my bed. I shoved a few bills and the gold nugget into my pocket and went looking for Rexy.

I wandered around the town until I found several corrals off the main thoroughfare. I tramped around each one, whistling and calling for Rexy. There were dozens of black horses in those corrals. Nearly all were muddy, bleeding, and lame—survivors of the White Pass.

After a while I gave up hope of finding Rexy, but I reached out to a small black horse who looked somewhat like her. I thought if I could buy a horse, I would go White Pass and save time.

I expected to see the dealer soon, and he appeared.

"Wanna buy a horse, son?"

"How much?"

"Two hundred dollars," he said. "A bargain."

The black horse whinnied softly and nuzzled up

to me. She reminded me of Rexy. We would make good partners.

"I'll think about it," I said.

The dealer scoffed, "No gold, huh? Off my fence."

"But I have gold." I pulled the gold nugget from my pocket.

The dealer eyed the nugget greedily. "I can't change that," he snarled.

"I'll change it and come back," I said.

By this time several men had gathered around. I was glad to see that one was the minister on his horse. He was dressed all in black, except for a white collar and a big white sombrero.

"Caught a little horse thief?" one of the men called, moving in.

The minister dismounted. "What's all the commotion here?" he asked. He smiled kindly.

"This young cheechako is trying to steal a horse," the dealer said.

"I'm not," I said, and I handed him the gold nugget. "Take it. I'll take the black horse." I did not want a commotion—not in this town.

The dealer threw a rope over the horse's head and moved it from the corral. "She's yours."

The horse nuzzled up to me again. She was worth a golden egg. I turned to lead her away.

"Wait a minute," the minister said. "I think I can make change for you." He took out a roll of paper money from his pocketbook and gave it to the dealer for the gold nugget. Then he held out the nugget to me.

"No," I said, surprised. "I made a deal."

"I see an honest boy," the minister said. "And I want to reward him. The horse is yours."

I shook my head and started to move on, but he grabbed my arm and dropped the gold nugget into my pocket.

"I'm happy," he said. Then he turned to the horse dealer, who was eagerly counting the bills. "Are you happy?"

"I'm happy," the dealer said.

"That's what I want," the minister said. "For everyone to be happy. Don't deny me that, young man. Now you go your way—happy."

Not knowing what else to do in this unusual circumstance, I did what the minister said. I led the black horse down the muddy street, happy at my good fortune.

Suddenly shots rang out. I could not say from where they came, but I ducked. At the same time, someone grabbed me from behind and pushed me facedown in the mud.

When I scrambled to my feet and wiped the mud from my face, I could see no one. Nor my black horse. I just caught a glimpse of a dapple-gray horse turning a corner.

"Help," I called out.

No one helped me. No one was on the street. Finally, I walked away.

At supper Mrs. Pullen continued her monologue. "You'll love the Mounties, especially you girls. British, you know. They are so handsome in their wide-brimmed hats and their red jackets with brass buttons. Ask for a button for a souvenir. They'll give you one. Pop it right off their jackets. They are good men, those Mounties."

She went out to the kitchen and returned with a tureen of soup, still talking.

"Not like Soapy Smith," she said. "He acts like the most benevolent man in the world, but he is just the opposite. But in Skagway he is the law and the religion. His men are everywhere."

We all looked up.

"Everywhere except in this house," she said quickly.

"That's heartening," one of the stampeders said, lapping up his soup.

I remembered my gold nugget then. And I knew before reaching into my pocket that it was gone.

Mrs. Pullen droned on. "They fleece the greenhorns. Cheechakos, they call them. And they fleece the sourdoughs, those coming back from the goldfields. Everyone gets it both ways—coming and going. And Soapy Smith gets rich."

"Who can a poor girl trust these days?" Violet asked, wide-eyed.

Mrs. Pullen sighed. "You can trust a Mountie. Me and the Mounties."

"This—this gangster," I stammered. "This Soapy Smith—what does he look like?"

Everyone looked at me.

"What does he look like?" Mrs. Pullen repeated.

I nodded.

"I thought everyone knew that," she said. "He looks like a minister with a white sombrero. And he rides a dapple-gray horse."

I choked on my soup.

"Careful," Mrs. Pullen said. "First thing you know, someone will say I use horse meat in my soup. Everyone's doing it. Boil it up. Serve it up. When the men cramp up on the trail, they don't know what hit them."

Everyone stopped eating and looked at Mrs. Pullen.

She laughed. "Continue eating. Nobody's going to die from my cooking. Unless it's from overeating."

For two weeks while it snowed, I stayed at Mrs. Pullen's and chopped wood for board and room. I bought my ton of supplies from a proprietor she recommended with another part of Pa's savings.

I decided to go Chilkoot Pass and, with two of the men at Mrs. Pullen's, took my goods by scow to Dyea, an Indian village suddenly turned gold rush camp.

There was no wharf at Dyea and the heavy scow beached three miles from shore. We waited an hour for low tide, and then packers with horse-drawn wagons came over the sandy tidal flats to haul our freight to the Dyea Trading Company Warehouse.

I stored all my goods except one trail outfit, which I needed to keep out the north wind: a fur-lined mackinaw coat, fur-lined cap and gloves, and a pair of high-laced rawhide boots.

Every few days I walked on the overland trail to Dyea to check on my supplies—and to break in my boots.

I kept busy days. It was the evenings that were lonely. I stayed in my room, thinking of Pa. And feeling like a naive Sphinx.

Out in the parlor the Flower Girls and the stampeders socialized. They played Mrs. Pullen's gramophone, taking turns winding it until their arms must have ached.

They were crazy over the new ragtime music, and they danced to the "Mississippi Rag" until their feet must have ached too.

The other song they played was "Where Is My Wandering Boy Tonight?"—a mournful thing to hear every night with the wind howling outside and the tar paper flapping.

Oh, where is my boy tonight?
Oh, where is my boy tonight?
My heart o'er-flows, for I love him he knows.
Oh, where is my boy tonight?

I shut my bedroom door and rolled the rug up to the crack. But I still heard it. So I put on my new fur-lined cap with earflaps. And I read dime novels.

CHAPTER 4

I FIND A PARTNER

Snow fell for two weeks, and then it froze. I saw Tlingit packers heading for the mountains. And I followed.

In Dyea I stood in the doorway of the warehouse looking at my ton of goods piled high on the floor. Then I looked up at the towering mountains of Chilkoot Pass, disappearing into the clouds. And I said, "James Erickson, it's impossible."

Then I was determined to prove I could do it. It is some kind of streak that runs through the Ericksons, Pa always said.

In that ton of goods were 350 lbs. Crown flour, 150 lbs. bacon, 50 lbs. evaporated potatoes, 4 dozen tins Eagle Brand condensed milk, 8 lbs. Royal baking powder, 10 lbs. seedless raisins, 50 lbs. evaporated onions, and 2 lbs. citrus extract tablets—and salt and navy beans and lard. And a lot of other things I could not imagine eating.

It was all packed in fifty-inch-long oilskin bags to be carried on my back over those mountains into Canada. Just because the Mounties said so.

In addition to the food, there were mackinaw coats and flannel underwear and rubber boots and German wool socks. Plus a tent, a saw, a coffeepot, nails, ropes, matches, candles, graniteware plates and cups, a portable Gold Nugget Yukon stove, and a seven-foot-long Yukon sled. And, of course, a pick, a shovel, and a gold pan.

It all seemed unnecessary for temporary squatting. And just as soon as I could fill those canvas bags with gold nuggets, I would be leaving again.

"Tell that to the Mounties," a whiskered man next to me said.

"I will," I said, surprised. I hoped—since he had read my thoughts—that he might ask me to be his partner.

But he walked off. And since I could not tell the con men from the stampeders, I did not ask him.

Still, I wasn't going to stand around wishing. I tied my tent on my sled, hoisted a bag of supplies on my back, and took off. Along with twenty-five thousand others who were taking the same trail.

I had decided on the steep Chilkoot Trail—sixteen and a half miles—rather than the longer White Pass because I had no horse. Also, the Indian packers favored the Chilkoot. And, as Mrs. Pullen had advised, when they packed, I packed.

As I staggered up the trail alongside the other stampeders, the Indian packers glided effortlessly past us. With the aid of leather tumplines around their foreheads and shoulders, they balanced two-hundred-pound packs upon their backs.

The Tlingits were short, swarthy, and clever, and their drooping mustaches made them appear to be frowning all the time. I thought it possible, however, that, what with charging the stampeders fifty cents a pound for packing supplies, they could be smiling on the inside.

Regardless, when they approached us on the trail, swinging their thick walking sticks and frowning, we stampeders stepped aside.

The trail followed the frozen Dyea River upstream. The first few miles were easy going, more like a rough wagon road than a mountain trail, and we walked three and four abreast. Some of the men wearing heavy rubber boots, however, lost them in the deep ruts.

Along the trail tent cities appeared, offering food, liquor, and beds. The first of these was called Finnegan's Point. I stopped there for a bowl of beans and then hurried on my way.

From here the trail followed the river into a narrow canyon about fifty feet wide, which was cluttered with boulders and fallen trees—and more rubber boots.

A cold wind blew down the canyon, piercing through all our mackinaw jackets, causing tempers to flare. Anyone who blocked the narrow trail for any reason was simply pushed aside. There was a kind of madness that winter on the Chilkoot Trail.

I stopped at Canyon City, a huddle of tents in the middle of the gorge, eight miles from Dyea. I decided this would be my first relay point. I set up my tent between two trees and left my pack inside.

Then I hurried back down the trail to Dyea, pulling my sled and frowning like a Tlingit.

This was my pattern for most of the month of November. I made twenty trips, stacking my supplies in my tent at Canyon City. Each night I trudged back to Dyea and slept in a bunkhouse hotel.

The other November days were howling snow-storms, days that I spent in the bunkhouse. I watched the frowning Tlingits, and when they stopped packing, I stopped. Those stampeders who did not were found along the trail—frozen.

One day in mid-November I passed the dance-hall girls, sitting on a boulder with their boots off. I did not notice them at first because they were wearing pants, just like men. The skinny boy was with them too.

"Jamie," they called. "Come and sit with us." They waved their wet stockings.

"Can't stop now," I called back, and I walked on as fast as I could.

On my return trip they were a few miles farther along, sitting on another rock. They had apparently hired the Tlingits to pack their supplies, no doubt a ton of ruffled dresses in tin boxes.

"Jamie," they called again. "You are going the wrong way."

I stopped, deciding to give that mollycoddled boy one more chance. I was surprised when he spoke to me first.

"Are you eating in the trail cafeterias?" he asked.

I said sometimes.

"They serve horse meat," he said, "just like Mrs. Pullen said."

I said he would really have something to complain about if he tasted my navy beans.

He laughed.

Their supplies had been sent with the Indian packers, as I had thought, but he said his mother, the one called Violet, had bought a frying pan and some groceries at a trailside stand. And that night she was going to cook pancakes for all of them.

Talking about food made me hungry, so I said I must be on my way.

"See you in Dawson City," the girls called. "Come and see us. The Flower Girls."

"I will."

"If you go to any of the taverns along the trail," the boy called, "watch out for portraits with moving eyes."

"I'll do that," I called back.

As I ran down the trail, I felt envious of that boy, for no other reason, I suppose, than that his mother was going to cook pancakes for him that night.

Several times when I arrived at Canyon City, I noticed footprints, larger than my own, around my tent. I was not surprised, therefore, when one day a few of my canvas bags were missing.

I kept a knife handy on my belt. No one was going to steal my supplies and get away with it.

To reach my tent earlier the next day, I packed only twenty-five pounds and did not stop to eat beans at Finnegan's Point. As I approached my tent, I could see a figure inside wearing a backpack. I crept closer and watched him rummage through my bags, his back toward the entrance.

I sprang like a cat, grabbing his legs. He went down, completely surprised, and I sat on top of him. Trembling, I pulled out my knife and, reaching over his pack, held it to his neck.

"Let's talk," he whined.

"After you return my supplies," I said. "Or I will run outside now and alert the camp."

I think we both recognized each other at the same time.

"James, s-son," he sputtered. "It's your old dad here."

It was Mr. Con Man from the *Guardian*.

I slid off his back, and he rolled over and sat up. We both sat looking at each other.

"I didn't know this was your tent, son," he said quickly. His beady eyes darted toward my knife and then toward the entrance to the tent.

"You won't tell on your old dad, will you? I'm just trying to make a living like everyone else. You'll have a little mercy, eh?"

"Don't call me 'son,'" I said, gripping the knife.

"Besides," he continued, "I was just paying a visit. Sorry I surprised you so."

"You're a thief."

Mr. Con Man flinched. "Grub snatcher. But you won't advertise it, will you, son, out there? You don't know what they do to grub snatchers in these camps."

"I know," I said.

"You won't, though?"

I did not say. And suddenly, he darted for the entrance.

I jumped up and lunged with my knife. Angry as I was, I was glad it slashed only his backpack. But what I saw shocked me as much as if it had been blood.

Feathers.

Then I realized the backpack was part of his disguise—a pack full of feathers, with little weight. He was too lazy to be a real stampeder.

As he ran down the trail, feathers blew out behind him like a goose being plucked in a blizzard.

I sat in my tent and laughed.

By November 25 all my supplies were cached in my tent at Canyon City, with a tunnel in the middle for me to crawl into with my sleeping bag. On one side of the entrance was my portable stove, its pipe extending through the tent top, and on the other side a stack of firewood. I planned to sleep in my tent during my relays to the next station, Sheep Camp, and I did not plan to freeze to death.

I stayed five days at Canyon City because of a storm. The snow pressed my tent down around my supplies until it looked like an igloo. I spent most of each day digging out and then digging back in. And trying to dry my wool socks.

I was so lonely in that tent that I started going to the taverns in the evenings just to be around someone. There were several in Canyon City, crowded with sweating men, no doubt as lonely as me.

I went to a different one each night. I stood near the stoves, watching the men drink and play faro, watching them gamble and lose.

After I was good and warm, I would find a portrait on the wall and stand with my back against it. I could hear those con men behind the removable eyes cussing me. I suppose one was my old pal Mr. Con Man, known to me now as Feathers. And, also, I suppose that was the reason I was not thrown out into the snow.

The snow really never stopped falling, but during a lull I saw the Indian packers starting out for Sheep Camp—five miles of steep, winding, boulder-strewn trail. And with a pack on my back and shovel in hand, I followed.

Sheep Camp was a flat spot on the side of the mountain that had earlier been a camping site for hunters of mountain sheep. Now it was another clutter of tents and shacks squeezed together on the banks of the narrowing Dyea River.

I had difficulty finding a place to stack my supplies and had to climb to the northern end of the camp before I found one. As I stood there looking up the mountain, the clouds parted and I caught a glimpse, far up, of the small notch of Chilkoot Pass.

I did not know how I could ever haul a ton of goods over that mountain. But I knew I could not give up now. If the frowning Tlingits could do it, so could a stubborn Viking.

To mark my place, I tied a shirt to my shovel and stuck it down in the snow beside my bags. I hurried back down the ragged trail as fast as I could, anxious to get back to my tent before dark.

Suddenly I heard my name. "James Erickson."

It was the skinny boy, sitting on a snowdrift at the side of the trail. He looked as cold as an icicle.

"Hello," I said. "Didn't see you. Where are the others?"

"Ahead. I'm catching up. Which way are you going?"

"Down," I said, "to Canyon City. How did you get separated?"

There was such a long silence that I knew something was wrong. "What happened?" I asked.

"My mother took sick," he said quietly. "We were clear up to the Scales, almost to the summit. But she was too sick to go on. We came back here to Sheep Camp because there is a doctor here."

He looked down. "She did not get better. It was spinal meningitis."

I did not know what to say. It was a horrible death, I knew. Even deep in my tent at Canyon City

I had heard screaming in the night from that killer. The first time, I thought I had dreamed it, until I heard someone say, "It was spinal meningitis last night."

"I am sorry about your mother," I said.

"Pansy said we would leave the next morning," the boy continued. "But the next morning when I woke up, they were gone."

"How long ago?"

"Last week before the snowstorm. I think they are waiting for me at the Scales, but this is the first day the trail has been open. I'll catch up with them soon."

I knew, and I suppose he knew, that you never catch up with someone who doesn't want you. But it was too difficult to say.

"Why don't you go back home?" I asked. "To Juneau. Where you got on the ship."

"Juneau isn't my home," he said, "any more than Sheep Camp. We traveled." He was about to cry, poor kid.

"While you are looking for your friends," I said, "do you want to join up with me? I relay my supplies, so I'm slow. You could help me. Or just be a tent-sitting partner. Doesn't matter."

He said yes so fast that I did not know what to say next.

"W-well," I stammered, "what's your name?"

"Tip."

"James," I said, shaking his cold, wet mitten.

I had a partner. Skinny, and not very tough—
but a partner. Named Tip.

• CHAPTER 5 •

OVER CHILKOOT PASS

That night I lay in my sleeping bag, smiling. I had a partner! Now I could pack twice as much, reach the goldfields twice as fast, and collect double the gold.

My new partner talked a lot from his sleeping bag.

"I can pay my own way," he blurted out. "I have my mother's savings—here in my knapsack."

That was good.

"And our supplies were carried by Indian packers to the summit. All paid for. Just waiting for me."

That was good too.

The next morning when I put a fifty-pound pack on my partner's back, he collapsed to the ground.

"How old are you?" I asked.

"Thirteen."

I took off twenty-five pounds. Still he could not stand up.

"And I'm a girl," he said, and burst into tears.

I should have known she was a girl—with a name like Tip.

"That's all?" I asked. "Tip?"

"The whole thing is Tzipporah Timothy Trattner."

"Is it a flower?"

"Of course it isn't a flower." She looked at me as if I had the peculiar name. "Why do you think it's a flower?"

"Well, Daisy and Petunia—"

"Oh." She laughed. "Those are their stage names. They are actresses, you know."

Tip dressed as a boy because her mother had felt it was safer, at least until they reached Dawson City. That explained her earlier actions, but still I was disappointed.

She was a green-eyed, skinny girl with black hair cut Dutch like a boy's. Named Tzipporah.

"I am named after my grandmother," she explained, "so I will grow up to be like her."

"What is your grandmother like?" I asked, hoping for an Amazon.

"I don't know," she said. "I have never met her."

"Can you talk less and walk faster?" I asked.

"Oh, sure." She broke into a run, stumbled, and lost her pack. I was beginning to see my dream of gold fading.

Next she was telling me about the song-and-dance routines of the Flower Girls, which did not interest me at all.

"My mother would not let me go on stage with the group," she said. "She was saving money so we could both go into legitimate theater. Anyway, that was our plan."

I nodded. Pa and I had had plans too. We were not going to be hack drivers forever. We were saving for a ranch like the one in Rock Springs. Only we would be the owners, not the hired hands.

"You should have seen my mother," Tip said, "when she sang on stage. She wore a long gown covered with pink roses, and she sat in a swing. Someone behind the curtain pulled it with a rope. People loved it. I suppose Pansy will sit in the swing now. Oh, well—"

We trudged up the trail. Tip singing soulfully:

After the ball is over,
After the break of morn,
After the dancers' leaving,
After the stars are gone;

Many a heart is aching,
If you could read them all;
Many the hopes that have vanished,
After the ball.

I set up my tent at Sheep Camp, and Tip and I packed my supplies there. It took a month. After the last trip I collapsed inside the tent.

My back ached, my feet ached, and I was cold. I crawled into my sleeping bag and covered my head, trying to block out the howling wind. I sensed Tip was doing the same, but I was too miserable to ask.

In the morning the tent was lying on top of us.

Tip was crying. "There is a hotel," she said, pulling on my sleeping bag. "Follow me. I'm paying."

During the four-day storm, we stayed at Palmer's Hotel with other stampeders. The hotel was a single room with one corner curtained off for Mr. and Mrs. Palmer and their children. Behind that curtain Mrs. Palmer cooked all day long, offering coffee, beans, and bacon for seventy-five cents.

Each evening the stampeders rolled out on the floor, after they hung their wet wool stockings from the rafters. Tip said she was going to choke to death. But I slept fine.

During the days we listened to Mr. Palmer talk. This was no trail for animals, he told us, although many stampeders managed to get them to this point. Here they were turned loose to starve or to be shot when they became a nuisance.

Tip and I were eating breakfast the first time we heard shots.

"Just putting some horses out of their misery,"
Mr. Palmer said.

From Sheep Camp we packed three miles to the
Scales, a flat shelf at the very base of the pass. Here
the Indian packers reweighed their loads on primi-
tive scales and doubled their prices. Now, at last,
they had something to smile about.

It was a difficult climb on packed snow to the
Scales. Each morning Tip and I squeezed into the
dark line of stampeders and plodded upward. It
took fifteen days to get all my supplies there.

Feathers would have loved the Scales. The same
things I had been packing for over two months
were strewn along the trail, free for the taking.
Plus live chickens in crates, trunks of clothing,
brass beds, mirrors, glassware, guitars, tin tubs,
umbrellas, and canoes. Almost anything a person
could want—if he could pack it.

But since it was all above timberline—and
firewood—I don't suppose Feathers ever made it
to the Scales.

The most difficult stretch of the entire trail was the
last half mile from the Scales to the summit, a steep
climb on ice. Earlier the Indian packers had hacked
steps into the ice, like a stairway, and the stampeders
followed. They called it the "Golden Stairs."

Tip and I joined the long dark line. We inched our way upward, grasping each step with our hands, hoping we would not slip. Every few yards shelves had been cut into the snow where we could step out and rest, but we did not want to leave the line for fear we would not get back in.

About halfway up Tip stopped. She would not move forward, and she could not move back.

"Keep going," I whispered. I pushed her legs with my head.

"Keep going!"

"I can't move," she cried. "I'm going to fall backward."

"Push him off!" the man behind me yelled.

I pulled her off onto a shelf, and we clung to each other like two scared mountain goats.

Tip said she was never going to move again. But after a while she realized that standing there was worse than climbing. We squeezed back into the line and climbed those fifteen hundred steps to the summit.

Going back down was faster. We sat on a slide called the "grease trail." And pushed off. We reached the bottom in just a few minutes.

Tip ran ahead to our tent, crawled inside, and said she was never coming out. I had heard that before. But I felt sorry for her. I told her that since her supplies were already at the summit, she was under no obligation to haul mine there.

She agreed.

I struggled up the steps each day. I could not afford the Indian packers, nor could I afford the new tramway that was now moving above my head.

But I would survive. I still had part of Pa's savings in my pocket, though none to waste.

As I pushed into the line, I tried not to get behind someone packing a shovel or a whipsaw. Awkward loads caused problems for the man behind, and no one helped a man with a problem except his own partner. And mine was hiding in my tent.

Therefore, I was surprised one morning when Tip strapped a pack onto her back and headed for the stairs. I said nothing, just stepped in line behind her.

The next morning, as we inched our way up the steps, I tried to thank her.

"From what I know of the family," I said, "I'd say you have a pretty nice grandmother."

"Thanks," she said, breathlessly. "I like going down the grease trail."

After our portable stove was packed up to the summit, Tip and I spent our last night at the Scales in a tent hotel. The floor was so crowded we had to roll a couple of sound sleepers onto their sides to make room for our sleeping bags. Tip held her nose and said she was going to choke to death—wet socks from the rafters again.

"It's our last climb up the stairs tomorrow," I whispered. The men snored around us. "Our last climb."

"I will beat you to the top too," she whispered back.

"By two or three steps."

When I awoke next morning, Tip was gone. I thought she would be waiting outside, but she was nowhere in sight. I searched that tent city in double-quick time, but still I could not find her.

Then I remembered what she had said about beating me to the top. I was furious with her. I stomped over to the trail and pushed into the line.

It was a stampeder on one of the shelves who saw her first. He was pointing and hollering. Finally I looked up.

She was high in the air, riding a swinging sled up the new tram. She lay facedown on the sled with her arms hanging over.

"Stop! Stop the tram!" I yelled.

"Keep moving!" The man behind me jabbed me with his walking stick.

I scrambled onto a shelf and waved frantically. "Hold on, Tip. Hold on!"

"Don't make him look down," a man in line said. "He could fall off."

"Pulleys don't hold too good," another man drawled. "Pulleys break. Fool man. He'll get kilt for sure."

"Just so he don't fall on me," the other man said. "One less for the gold."

I shut my eyes and prayed.

At the summit I did not have to look far. She was standing next to the machine gun blocking the narrow passageway to Canada, waving wildly like the Union Jack above her.

"You crazy fool," I yelled. "I'll bet your grandmother's a crazy fool too!"

"I beat you," she said proudly. "And I have already passed customs. The Mounties said my mother's supplies—and mine—were packed all the way down to Lake Bennett. Nice chaps, they are. And look—" She held out a brass button.

I just stood there speechless.

Several times on my relay trips I had looked down at the other side of the mountain. It was almost as steep as the American side, with a dark line of men struggling down as precariously as they had struggled up.

I had heard about another trail, one that the Indians used. After my supplies had been checked, I asked one of the Mounties about it.

"Next to impossible," he said. "The Indians slide down with all their baggage at breakneck speed. Once they start, it is impossible to stop. Highly risky, even for a Tlingit."

I did not mention the danger of the trail to Tip. I just dragged my sled over there and worked fast.

I piled on all my supplies. I covered them with canvas and tied them securely. Then I tied the tent behind the sled.

"We lie down on the tent and hold on to the sled," I instructed my partner. "Scream all the time so others can move out of our way."

For a moment I looked back down Chilkoot Pass. I had climbed that mountain for two and a half months, and I was tired of climbing. And I was only sixteen and a half miles closer to the gold.

As I stood there, the gold suddenly seemed not so important. I had climbed Chilkoot Pass. Nothing could ever be impossible again.

Tip was on her stomach, clutching the back of the sled. Her eyes were shut tight.

"Ready?" I shouted.

"Ready." She began screaming.

I gave the sled a mighty push and jumped onto the tent next to Tip. We were off.

CHAPTER 6

ON THE SHORES OF LAKE BENNETT

We hit bottom about ten minutes later and shot out onto the rough ice of Crater Lake.

"Drag!" I yelled. "Stop screaming and drag your feet!"

When we finally came to a stop, Tip rolled off the canvas, stunned. "Now what?" she gasped.

"Now we get ourselves off this volcanic crater," I said. I looked around for the stampeders' trail. It was not hard to spot—the same dark line moving down the mountainside.

"We are ahead of somebody, for once," I said, pulling at Tip. "Let's get going."

Tip staggered to her feet. "If all those stampeders drag their feet like we did," she said, "they will all end up inside this crater."

"They won't," I said, "because they won't come down this way. Just us—and the Tlingits."

We pulled our loaded sled over small frozen lakes

and down a twisting canyon to Lake Lindeman, the first mountain lake where navigation to the Yukon River would begin in the spring. On top of the snow, men were already felling trees and hammering together boats for the last lap of the journey to Dawson City, a five-hundred-mile distance.

At Lake Lindeman we stopped to rest, then pressed on to Lake Bennett, where Tip's supplies had been packed. I told myself, as I forced my legs to keep moving, that in the spring we would be several miles ahead of all those stampeders at Lake Lindeman.

When we arrived, we dragged our sled along the shores of Lake Bennett, looking for a spot big enough to pitch our tent. It was here that the White Pass and the Chilkoot Pass trails converged, creating another crowded tent city.

Finally we found a good spot, a flat area in a wooded cove with a forest of pines and poplars rising behind. Looking at some of the other tents, squeezed between the trees, we felt lucky.

"From here on," I said to Tip, "it is easy going. We just sit in a boat and float down the mighty Yukon for five hundred miles."

Tip looked around. "I don't see any mighty Yukon."

"It starts right here," I explained. "From the ice of Lake Bennett, in the spring. We just sail a boat from one lake to another and down one or two little rivers, and soon it turns into a wide river. Then it is called the mighty Yukon."

I could hardly believe it myself. No more hiking. No more packing. Just sailing a boat to Dawson City, getting out, and picking up the gold.

"I don't see any boat, either," Tip said. She looked straight at me with her big green eyes.

"The boats are still growing," I said, nodding toward the forest. "And we had better hang our tent from a couple, fast, before they are chopped down."

The next day we went to see the Mounties about Tip's supplies, which were somewhere in the tons of goods stacked around the lake. The Mounties knew just where they were, and they also knew about the Flower Girls.

The girls had been so anxious to reach Dawson City that they had paid an exorbitant amount to have the Indian packers take them on sleds over the ice-covered lakes and down the Yukon River. They had stayed at Lake Bennett only overnight.

"Do you think they made it all right?" Tip asked.

"With the Indian guides, I would say so," the Mountie answered. "Alone, no."

We found Tip's supplies and packed them to our tent. The food and hardware were intact, but the clothing was missing.

"My mother said something that night," Tip said quietly. "She said to get her white fox coat. 'Promise,' she said."

"I suppose it was the most expensive thing she had," I said.

Tip shook her head.

"Maybe she was delirious."

"She was not delirious," Tip said. "And she kept saying it. And I promised. I thought it would be here."

"We'll get it back," I said. "As soon as we get to Dawson City."

The first week at Lake Bennett, we chopped firewood and piled it outside our tent. In case of a big snow.

It snowed all right, for five days and nights without stopping. But since we did not have to pack anything anywhere, we loved it. We went sledding down through the pines, and we made snow angels halfway across Lake Bennett. Just before dusk we hurried back to our tent and pushed wood into our stove. And we made sourdough pancakes.

We got our sourdough starter from a stampeder named Big Red, who carried it in a flask around his neck. He packed with it and slept with it. He said it had never stopped bubbling since he'd gotten it in Skagway three and a half months before.

"Keep it warm," he said, pouring a little of the

precious leaven into our cup. "Treat it like a baby. Don't forget it."

We chopped a woodpile for that cup of fermented dough, twenty quaking aspen trees cut into blocks to fit into Big Red's stove. We were not likely to be careless with it.

Every night we added a little flour and water to the starter. In the morning we added a pinch of salt and a pinch of soda, taking out a cup for our next starter. Next we added as much flour as we wanted—thick for biscuits, thin for pancakes.

We mostly made pancakes, burned ones, soggy ones, until we caught on to the air holes on top, indicating when to flip them over. Then we made the best sourdough pancakes in all of Canada.

And every night, like Big Red, I took the starter to bed with me.

"Do you know how to build a boat?" Tip shouted.

I had just chopped down a spruce tree, which had barely missed a hillside tent. No, I did not know how to build a boat, but neither did most of the other men scattered around the lake. They just chopped down trees and dragged them down the mountains. And cussed. And fought at the saw pits.

The saw pits were elevated platforms for sawing the logs into lumber. One man stood up on the platform and held one handle of a six-foot saw, while his partner beneath grasped the lower handle. As they pulled up and down, the man below was showered with sawdust. As a result, many partnerships were dissolved.

I picked up two oars cheap from two partners who were fighting, and not because of the sawdust. They had carried a prefabricated canoe over Chilkoot Pass and all they had to do now was nail it together. But in anger, they sawed their canoe in half and divided their supplies. I bought one oar from one partner and one oar from the other. And each one tried to sell me half a canoe.

"Do you," Tip called again, "know how to build a boat?"

I swung my ax mightily as I trimmed the fallen spruce tree.

"I am not named Erickson for nothing," I replied. "Ever hear of Leif Ericson, the mighty Viking?" I crossed my fingers as I stretched the truth. "He's my grandfather."

I had planned to build a flat-bottomed scow, like most of the other men, chopping spruce trees and slicing them into planks at the saw pits. But I shuddered when I watched the men at the saw pits. Even the strongest of partners had problems there.

I glanced around for my partner. She was sitting up in an old cottonwood tree, singing like a bird. I could hear her above the whining of the saws:

My sweetheart's the man in the moon,
I'm going to marry him soon. . . .

I kicked the tree, suddenly angry with the partner that fate had chosen for me.

The tree looked as if it would topple over at any moment, its long branches leafless and dry, reaching out over the frozen lake.

I stepped back quickly. Its long branches *were* leafless and dry. And lightweight. Laughing aloud, I ran headlong for the cottonwood tree. We could forget the saw pits. We would build a raft!

During the next few days we found many dry cottonwood trees. We cut and trimmed fifteen logs, which we dragged down to the ice. We decided to build the raft on the ice, so when it thawed the raft would already be in the water.

We laid the logs side by side with the longest ones in the middle. It looked like a raft already.

We laid three poles across and lashed them with rope to the logs beneath. Before we were finished,

we ran out of rope, but we were able to trade supplies for more.

In the weeks that followed, I carved a steering
oar for the stern and made a steering post from a
forked tree branch. And I carved a long slender log
for poling.

Later on we fastened a short mast to the raft and
made a sail from some canvas in Tip's supplies.

One day I found a man who was willing, for five
pounds of sugar, to cut a log into thin planks for a
deck on our raft. I began nailing them to the cross
poles while Tip watched.

"Oh, a dance floor!" she exclaimed. She started
dancing the cancan in her rubber boots.

"N-not exactly," I stuttered. "It's to keep the
water from splashing up between the logs."

As we worked on the raft, the days gradually
became longer. The snow began to melt from the
mountainsides and wildflowers burst into bloom—
purple crocuses and bluebells. Geese honked overhead, returning home. Spring was coming to the
North.

By the end of April the raft was finished. We
christened her *El Dorado*, because she would take
us to our land of gold. We waved her name from a
flag on top of the mast for all the world to see.

I was proud of that raft.

During the month of May I slept on the raft, just

to keep an eye on her. One night as I was looking up into the starry sky, I asked right out loud,
"What do you think of this raft, Pa? What do you
think?"

He did not need to answer, because I knew he
liked it just fine.

The ice held through May, melting during the
daytime, freezing again at night. The Mounties
called it "anchor ice," and warned everyone
against it.

Still, one stampeder went out. He said no
Englishman in a fancy red jacket could tell him to
keep off the ice. He was quite a distance out before
the Mounties noticed him. They yelled at him to
come back. We all yelled. But he just kept walking,
daring the ice.

Suddenly he screamed and reached desperately
toward shore. Then he disappeared through the
ice. There was nothing anyone could do, not even
the Mounties.

I went back to my tent, trying to forget what I
had seen.

After that the men were not quite so impatient.
They sat in their makeshift boats—floating coffins,
the Mounties called them—and waited. And cussed.
At last, on May 29, the ice broke and, before it had
completely moved out, the boats moved in.

It was a wild parade: scows crashing into the

floating ice, skiffs dodging each other, canoes overturning, and rafts sinking as soon as they left shore.

Tip jumped aboard our raft, swinging the oars and yelling at all colliding boats. I stood shoreside in rubber boots, talking to the raft as if she were a horse. Finally I gave a great push and crawled over the wet logs.

For a minute I thought the *El Dorado* was going to sink. But she just dipped low and turned slowly around.

I grabbed an oar, and Tip and I both rowed as fast as we could.

"We're going in circles," Tip called.

"She is just looking around," I said. I was so proud of that raft, it did not matter to me which direction she went. Just so she stayed afloat.

• CHAPTER 7 •

DOWN THE MIGHTY YUKON

We crossed Lake Bennett in circles. And after most of the boats had passed us, we renamed our raft *El Turtle*.

"What do you think she's dragging?" Tip asked. She crawled to the stern and leaned over. "Something like a boulder?"

"Something like a continent," I said.

That started us laughing. We laughed so hard we could not row. We just sat on the deck, looking around. And when we looked at each other, we started laughing again.

"What's so funny?" a passing boatman called.

We were laughing too hard to answer.

He dropped down onto his stomach and tried to look under his boat. "Fool kids," he yelled.

We tried to go north. We rowed, and we poled, and I stood at the stern working the steering oar. When a wind came up, we raised sail and were blown back almost to where we had started from.

Other stampeders, we noticed, were adding centerboards to their boats. And we did the same. We cut a board from our deck planks and slipped it between the middle logs near the center. It could be pulled up or down according to the depth of the water.

At last we were headed north. It was evening by this time, however, and when we spotted a sandy beach in a cove, we steered the raft toward it.

We ended up about a mile farther down in a glacial mud deposit. We waded ashore, sinking to our boot tops, and were met by black swarms of mosquitoes. We hurried back to the raft, the mosquitoes in pursuit.

The outfitter at Skagway had insisted on mosquito netting and eucalyptus oil. I had doubted his word, but now I frantically sought those supplies, which were at the bottom of our stack of goods.

We pushed hard and fast to free the raft from that swamp. And even then the mosquitoes followed us out to the current.

After that we went ashore only when we needed wood for our stove, which we had set up on deck, or when a storm forced us there. Otherwise lowered our sail and slept on deck, floating along in the Northern twilight until we bumped into something.

Our raft was always bumping into things on those glacial lakes—Lake Bennett, Lake Tagish, and Lake Marsh. Things like ice floes and snags. We spent several nights on sandbars, but we did not care. There were no mosquitoes in the middle of a lake. Fish jumped all around for our supper. And there was always the next day for digging out. We were king and queen of our world, even though that world was only ten by eighteen feet.

The Queen of the Raft was a real talker. And the only person she had to talk to was me.

This is how she would begin a conversation:

"I've been thinking today about my dear aunt who died of a broken heart."

"Oh?" I would say.

"Yes, you see, there was this tavern in her town where her husband used to sit down and drink wine. Well, one night he saw a damsel dark, and they started to spark."

"He wasn't true to his wife?"

Tip would shake her head sadly. "He was not true. After that my aunt would not play her harp anymore. Not for anyone. She hung it up on a willow tree—and died."

"You don't say."

"And," Tip would whisper, fighting back the tears, "on her tombstone they carved a turtledove to signify she died of love."

And just as I was about to believe it, she would burst out singing:

There is a tavern in the town, in the town,
And there my dear love sits him down,
  sits him down,
And drinks his wine 'mid laughter free,
And never, never thinks of me.

We laughed until our sides ached. And the passing boatmen would holler, "What's up?"

We would answer, "Can't say. We are going downstream."

I did not know any Tin Pan Alley songs, nor did I have the gift for making things up. The only story I knew was true, about Pa and the traveling dentist, when Pa said, "Next time, apply the anesthetic first."

But it served the purpose. After a while I simply had to say, "Once my pa had a toothache," and we laughed just as hard as when I told the whole story.

Boats passed us every day, still coming from Lake Bennett and the higher Lake Lindeman. We slowed some of them down by waving them over to us.

"Which way to Dawson City?" I would call.

Or Tip would shout, "Can you tell us the reason for this stampede?"

"Fool kids!" the men would yell, livid at wasting a few minutes.

The stampeders quarreled in their boats, just as they had on land. One man was left on a sandbar, waving and cursing as his partner sailed away. Finally some Indians noticed him and rowed out in their canoes to save him.

We laughed at these antics from the safety of our small world.

One night we camped on a high bank of Lake Marsh because we needed firewood. Since it was high and rocky, the mosquitoes did not bother us. The next morning I unpacked my rifle, which I had bought at Lake Bennett, and went into the forest to hunt. I was hunting moose, but I ended up picking wild raspberries and onions.

The queen gathered flowers—blue lupines and bluebells, pink wild roses, yellow arctic poppies, and scarlet fireweed. And she decorated the raft.

She said we looked like one of those floating gardens down in Mexico. I thought we looked more like a floating coffin, but I did not say so.

I watched her weave a ring of pink roses in her hair, and then admire herself in the emerald lake.

"Are you turning back into a girl now?" I asked. I always thought of her as a girl, although she still dressed as a boy. We were less conspicuous that way.

She smiled, then shook the flowers into the water.

"It isn't permanent, you know," I added hopefully.

"I know," she said. "My mother thought it best, at least until I get to Dawson City."

"Then what?" I asked a question that I had been avoiding. "When you get to Dawson City?"

"You mean—am I going to join the Flower Girls, or stay partners with you?"

"Yes, I guess that is what I mean."

"You don't like the Flower Girls?"

"They ditched you. And your grandmother Tzipporah and I do not like that."

She laughed a little.

I asked another question I had avoided. "Are you planning to be a dance-hall girl?"

"Don't you think I am pretty enough?"

I stared at her straggly cropped hair and bony features. And ragged clothes. I guess her large green eyes were the only feature I had particularly noticed before.

"You'll do," I said, "with a few ruffles and pearls. But"—I hesitated—"are you sure you want to be a dance-hall girl?"

"What else could I be? I already know the songs."

"After we get to Dawson City and pick up the

gold," I said, "you can be anything you want. Because you will have the money to pay for it. School, business, Nob Hill mansion—anything."

"I think I will be an actress in the legitimate theater, then," Tip said. She whirled a pink rose in the water. "Or have an orphanage. What about you?"

I had never told anyone my dream, except Pa. And I hesitated.

"Well, don't worry that I will tell anyone," Tip said. "We don't have many visitors on this raft."

"It has something to do with horses," I said. "Maybe own a ranch with horses, like the one I worked on in Wyoming. Or be a veterinarian. I don't know yet." I slapped at a couple of mosquitoes that had found us.

"Let's push off this floating garden," I said, "or the gold will all be gone before we get there."

We jumped off, pushed from the rocks, and climbed back on board. The blossoms that fell from the raft danced in the rippling mint-green water.

We had heard about Miles Canyon from the Mounties at Lake Bennett. In fact, I had drawn a rough map of the route to Dawson City from their descriptions.

The upper Yukon was a series of lakes connected

by rivers. Miles Canyon was midway along Fifty Mile River, which linked Lake Marsh to Lake Laberge.

At the canyon, between walls of dark basalt, the river narrowed to one third its previous size. In its center was a whirlpool. From this point on, the river constricted further, to only thirty feet across.

The upper Yukon waters gushed through this narrow passage and burst out into two sets of rapids—the Squaw Rapids, rushing over a series of jutting rocks, and then the White Horse Rapids, where water sprayed into the air like leaping white stallions.

"Look for a piece of red calico tied to a tree," I said to Tip. "And then a sign that reads 'Cannon.'"

"But what do we do?"

"We beach and portage our raft and supplies around the canyon, about five miles through the forest."

"We can't do that," Tip exclaimed.

"Or," I continued, reading my notes, "hold to the crest of the current."

"We will do that," Tip said. "We will hold to the crest of the current."

We heard the rapids, like rolling thunder, but we could not tell how far away they were. After a turn in the river, Tip spotted the red calico tied to a leaning tree, then the board with CANNON scrawled across it.

I was having second thoughts, but it was already too late to change our minds. The mighty river had lifted our craft like a twig and was carrying it recklessly onward.

I leaned against the steering oar with all my strength, trying to guide the raft. It broke with a loud snap, and I fell to the deck.

"Lower the centerboard all the way," I called to Tip. I grabbed the steering pole and plunged it into the raging water, although I knew it was a futile attempt.

"Let's portage," Tip screamed.

"Get down and hold on," I yelled. "If we slip from the crest and head for the rocks, jump off and swim."

"I can't swim," Tip yelled.

I could not swim either. Before the Yukon, all the water I had ever seen was in watering troughs— that is, until I saw the Pacific Ocean, which I was not counting.

The raft plunged up and down, twisting toward the rock walls and then toward the gaping whirlpool. It creaked and groaned. Water sprayed into our faces, blinding us.

Our portable stove slid past me and off the raft.

It bobbed a minute in the water and then sank out of sight.

Suddenly, with a great surge, we were spewed out of the narrow gorge. We had ridden the river through Miles Canyon!

Then all at once, before we had time to look about, we were shooting over white rapids and twisting around black rocks.

"We are going to hit!" Tip screamed.

The raft grazed the side of a jagged rock, throwing us across the deck. It rattled for a moment and then plunged forward.

Below the rapids we still clutched the raft, unable to believe the calm.

"Is it over?" Tip asked, looking up.

"That was Squaw Rapids," I said. "The small ones. Let's beach and portage like the Mounties said. This raft will split up if it goes through any more rapids."

"I will split up," Tip exclaimed.

I looked around. The river was strewn with timber and wreckage. Stampeders crouched on rocks and huddled on the shore.

According to the map, it was about two miles before the White Horse Rapids. I planned to beach the raft before then.

I discovered my rope had washed overboard along with the stove. And the steering pole and oars. In desperation I pulled a rope from the supplies, which were still tied down securely.

I made a lasso and whirled it at projecting rocks near the shore. I missed. I called frantically to other boatmen, but they gestured helplessly. They, too, were at the mercy of the river.

Then I saw the White Horse Rapids, spraying white foam high into the air. They looked like wild, leaping stallions.

At that moment, for some unknown reason, the rapids beckoned to me. I had no desire to beach the raft. I wanted to plunge into the middle of those wild horses and ride them to the finish.

"Hold on, Tip," I shouted. "We're going through!"

Our raft was carried by the white horses, first on one back, then another. Sometimes we faced upstream, sometimes down. We were at the mercy of the wild white horses.

I saw the boulder on the right just before we hit it, but there was nothing I could do. I heard the loud cracking of logs and the snapping of rope. And I wondered how fast I could learn to swim.

The raft shuddered and pitched violently. Then, as if knowing it had had enough, it righted itself, and scraped over a gravel bar into shallow water. We were beached.

I lay limp as seaweed, my face pressed against

the wet logs. I wiggled my toes, my feet, my arms. I looked up, wiping water and sand from my face.

Tip was sprawled out beside me, looking dazed.

"We did it!" she sputtered.

I dragged myself from the raft and surveyed the damage. The outside log, right side, was cracked and the bow rope broken. The raft was stripped of everything except our bags of supplies, which were still tied down. And the two of us.

"I'm not named Erickson for nothing," I shouted, and I collapsed on the cold wet sand.

CHAPTER 8

CITY OF GOLD

Tip and I spent several days at the White Horse Rapids repairing our raft. We found two oars and a pole that had washed ashore, possibly our own, but we had to trade twenty-five pounds of bacon for a steering oar.

We made a new mount for the steering oar from wreckage strewn about, but we did not replace the mast and sail. We would depend upon the river's current for the remainder of the journey.

Daily we checked the beach for our stove, but if it washed ashore, we never found it. We traded our last bottle of eucalyptus oil for a stove from a man who had three.

"No doubt our own," Tip said, sighing.

I did not complain, however, because our supplies were intact.

"I knew a man once," I told Tip, "named Feathers."

I smiled, remembering. "He would love it here. This is his kind of place."

We pushed off for Lake Laberge, the last of the Yukon lakes, after which rivers flowed all the way to Dawson City and on to the Bering Sea.

"Any more rapids?" Tip asked.

"Just a couple of little ones," I said, checking my worn map. "About a hundred miles from here. Five Finger Rapids and Rink Rapids. Nothing to worry about."

On Lake Laberge, as on Lake Marsh, we spent a lot of time on gravel bars. We talked about the gold, and we fished for grayling. I was glad when Tip said she was sick of fish, as it gave me an excuse to go hunting again. One morning early we poled the raft over to the shore. I wrapped myself in mosquito netting, grabbed my rifle, and took off into the woods.

"I will return with game," I said.

There were animals in the woods—moose, bear, caribou, and rabbits. I had seen them from the raft. Now I could see only their tracks in the damp earth.

Finally, I sat down under a clump of quaking aspens with my rifle cocked, and I waited.

After a while a red squirrel ran down the trunk of a spruce tree, darted in front of me, and scampered up another tree. I fired once.

I ran back to the raft, spattered with mud and pursued by hordes of mosquitoes. But victorious. At least I was smarter than a red squirrel.

Because of the mosquitoes, we pushed offshore and floated slowly down the clear green waters of Lake Laberge. While I had been hunting, the queen had again decorated the raft with woodland flowers. And as we rowed out, a trail of fragrant blossoms followed in our wake.

"I'll cook supper tonight," I said proudly. "You just putter around in the garden." I skinned and cleaned the squirrel, and I put it to soak in salted water.

Tip eyed it suspiciously as it soaked in the frying pan. "Do you know how to cook squirrel?" she asked.

"Of course," I answered, hoping Pa's old Wyoming rabbit recipe worked with Yukon squirrel. I rummaged through our supplies, looking for a can of evaporated onions.

That evening, drifting with the current down Lake Laberge, I cooked my first wild game—squirrel smothered in onions. The aroma from that frying pan outdid Wyoming rabbit. I was proud to share it with the queen.

The queen drew away in disgust. "It looks dead."

"It is," I said sharply. "Just like the fish we eat."

She lifted the squirrel with a fork, dangling it by one leg. "It looks murdered." She dropped it over the edge of the raft.

I lunged at her. "Get off," I yelled. "Get off my raft!"

I stomped over to a corner of the raft and turned my back on her. We were quarreling like adults.

I heard a splash, not much louder than a fish makes. And I knew Tip was in the water. I was sorry immediately, but that did not help. Tip could not swim. And I could not stop the raft.

"Grab the pole!" I yelled, holding it out to her. She missed it.

I was frantic. I wanted to jump in and save her. But I could not swim either.

"Help!" I cried, looking around for other boats.

Quickly I untied a rope from the supplies and threw it. "Grab it!" I yelled.

Her arms were flailing above the water, as thin and fragile as flower stems in the wind. As the rope skimmed the water, I prayed to God for her life. Then I saw her go under.

I pulled the rope, and she was holding on.

We never quarreled again.

The outlet from Lake Laberge was a narrow, twisting river called Thirty Mile. The boats we had missed on Lake Laberge were all bunching up here.

"You two boys still afloat?" one stampeder called as he rammed into us with his scow. "Thought we lost you back at Miles Canyon."

"No," I shouted. "We're in it for the gold."

That worried him, and he began shouting at his boat to go faster.

The Thirty Mile River began a series of rivers similar to the chain of lakes earlier—the Teslin, the Big Salmon, the Little Salmon, and the Lewes. On the cold, clear waters of the Lewes River were the rapids.

This time I was not taking any chances. I lassoed a stubby spruce and beached the raft miles before the Five Finger Rapids. I tied down our stove and all the oars, except the steering oar.

"You can walk around the rapids," I said to Tip. "No need for both of us to get wet."

"No thanks."

"You can follow along the riverbank," I said. "All the way—even at the rapids."

She shook her head.

"What's the matter?" I asked. "Bears?"

"No."

"What then?" I was trying hard to be patient. She had been asking about the rapids for days. Now she just sat on top of the supplies, hugging her knees, looking at me with her big eyes, the color of glacier water.

"You like them, don't you?" she asked. "Rapids."

I looked at her, surprised. "Yes. It's in my blood. How did you know?"

"Well"—she smiled broadly—"it's in mine, too."

We sailed fearlessly toward the Five Finger Rapids, four ominous black rocks towering in the middle of the river. The water surged around them in five channels—like fingers.

I grabbed the map in my pocket and read: HUG THE RIGHT CLIFF.

With all my strength I steered to the right. And we headed straight for the rock wall.

"We're going to hit," Tip screamed.

Just when I thought we would crash, a cross-current turned the raft and bounced it through the middle channel as if pulled by a rope.

I was speechless with fright.

Tip hollered, "Now how far to Rink Rapids?"

"I will ask the Mounties," I said, reaching for the crumpled map.

That started us laughing, and we laughed all the way to Rink Rapids, however far that was. We laughed as we pitched and bumped over the treacherous falls, I suppose because Tip was thirteen and I was now fifteen—and we were indestructible.

At last we reached the main stream of the Yukon River, wide and swift enough to carry us without oars or sail. For the rest of the journey to Dawson City we steered only to dodge islands. And laughed. And dreamed about the gold.

We had almost forgotten that others were also dreaming of the same gold, and as we drew closer to the City of Gold, the race became deadly.

Partnerships that had survived the Lake Bennett saw pits and the Yukon waterway were now dissolving. Men threw each other overboard, they sawed boats in half, and they fought onshore while their boats drifted away.

At the mouth of the Pelly, a tributary pouring into the Yukon, was a Split-Up Island. And a few miles downstream, near the Stewart, was a Split-Up City.

Tip and I watched partners, livid with anger, cutting sacks of rice and flour in half, their contents spilling out over the sand. One group laid out six blankets on the beach and divided all their supplies, pouring the contents of the sacks into big mixed-up piles. When the men realized their supplies were wasted, they ran around frantically, trying to find new partners.

Several men asked to hitch up with Tip and me, and they promised us everything. We said we were too slow.

It was a humorous sight, but sad. We did not laugh at the antics of those adults as we once had.

As the journey neared its end, all the stampeders held their crafts to the right bank, moving cautiously around each bend of the wide river. No one wanted to miss the City of Gold now.

Tip and I had not won the race with our raft, but neither had we lost. As far ahead as we could see, and as far back, the right bank of the river was lined with boats.

It was the end of June 1898. I had been on the gold trail for ten months. And I was 2,500 miles from where I'd started.

I remembered the old miner at the San Francisco harbor, dragging his heavy suitcases. I recalled the gold piece he had given me, and how I had lost it in Skagway. I would not be so foolish again, I vowed.

I looked at Tip, perched on top of the supplies, peering up the river. She would notify me, she said, when she spotted Dawson City. Her black bangs hung so long over her eyes that I wondered how she could see anything.

Slowly we sailed around a broad curve in the river, and there on the right the roaring Klondike River surged into the slower-moving Yukon. It forced our raft back into the middle of the river.

"Land ho!" Tip called, jumping from her crow's nest.

"Man the oars," I shouted. In my excitement, I stumbled over my own feet.

Just ahead at the junction of the two rivers, shimmering in a misty marsh, was the end of my rainbow, my City of Gold—Dawson City.

CHAPTER 9

WE STAKE A CLAIM

I was no stranger to life's surprises. Nor was Tip. Still, we were completely unprepared for the surprise at Dawson City. We were too late for the gold.

Tip and I. And forty thousand others who had survived the trek. But the bitter part was finding out that we had been too late before we started.

It had been almost two years since George W. Carmack and his two Indian companions had discovered gold on Rabbit Creek, renamed Bonanza Creek, on August 14, 1896. A year had passed before the outside world heard the news, the day I remembered so well, when the *Excelsior* arrived in the San Francisco harbor.

By that time the golden creeks of Bonanza and Eldorado had been staked by prospectors already in the North country and the lucky few who managed to reach there early in the autumn of 1897, before winter set in.

"What went wrong?" Tip asked. She stomped her muddy boots on the boardwalk.

We were pacing the boardwalks of Front Street, our hands deep in our pockets, our shoulders hunched as if we were freezing cold in July. We were trying to blame someone, just as the other disillusioned men shuffling at our side were doing.

"Hang the Mounties!" someone shouted.

"Hang the press!"

"Try President McKinley and the Spanish-American War!"

There was gold in Dawson City. It was piled high in the back rooms of the trading-company stores, waiting for the arrival of steamers from the Outside. Klondike kings flashed it as they paraded up and down Front Street with dance-hall girls on their arms and bottles of champagne in their pockets.

Tip and I stopped in front of the Pioneer Saloon, listening to one of the new ragtime tunes being pounded out on a piano.

"There's no one to blame, Tip," I said. "There never is. You just have to play your own trick back on everyone."

"What is your plan?" Tip put her hands on her skinny hips and looked me straight in the eye.

"No plan yet," I said. "But"—I lowered my

voice—"there is gold here. In the streams, in the hills, in sawdust floors, in kitchen sinks. And I will find it. And then I will leave—laughing."

I looked at my reflection in the window of the saloon.

"After I get a haircut," I added, trying to get a closer look. I pressed my face up to the glass and looked right into a round red face puffing a cigar.

Tip laughed.

"So"—I turned around—"are you going to make a million with me, or do you want to go find your dance-hall friends?"

"With you," Tip said.

Tip and I stayed in Dawson City several days, watching the carnival on Front Street: spielers calling out the names of dance-hall queens—Diamond Tooth Gertie and French Fanny; prospectors shuffling in and out of swinging doors as if hypnotized.

Once we found ourselves on Paradise Alley, where ladies of the evening, sitting at their windows, winked and waved at us. But mostly we stood around the gold recorder's office, listening for information.

One afternoon as I stood idly watching the crowd, someone grabbed me from behind, clutching me so I could hardly breathe. When I pulled one arm free, ready to swing at him, I saw who it was—Snorin' Sam from the steamer. He was just hugging me. That's how lonely it was in the North.

"Erickson," he exclaimed. "Good to see you. My, how you have grown."

"How long have you been here?" I asked. "And how did we both get here without passing each other?"

He said he and his two partners had gone White Pass Trail with horses, and they had built their boat below Lake Bennett. He had been in Dawson City two weeks.

Two weeks in Dawson City, and he knew everything.

The golden creeks of the Klondike River were already claimed, he said, and just a few weeks before we arrived, some lucky cheechakos had found gold in the foothills and started another stampede.

"However," Sam said, "every few days a rumor goes around about gold somewhere else—seventy-five, one hundred miles from here. And overnight half of Dawson disappears. Even the high-heeled dancing girls run out their back doors with lanterns and picks, and skip over the hills."

"Then what?" I asked.

"They all come creeping back. Once"—he chuckled—"once some stampeders began staking

Dawson City. All over private property. People found stakes pounded on their doorsteps and in their outhouses. The Mounted Police had to put a stop to it.

"Still," he continued, "you never know. That's how Bonanza and Eldorado started, and the golden hills."

He paused for breath. "You just have to keep your ears open, and then run.

"By the way," he added, "have you seen our cabinmate, the one on the bottom bunk?"

For a moment I thought maybe he was a con man, and my heart sank. He looked lean and desperate. But so did everyone else. I was still having trouble telling the cons from the regulars.

"I saw him on the Chilkoot Trail," I said. "Seems he was in the feather business. I think he turned back."

I decided Sam was regular, because he said, "Too bad."

"Yes," Tip said. She indicated the piles of goods for sale all over the muddy waterfront. "Your old friend would have loved it here."

Most of the latecomers, without ever seeing the goldfields, had put all their supplies up for sale, hoping to make enough money to return home on the first steamer coming in from the Bering Sea.

Sam told us more. "There is always a possibility

of a 'fraction,'" he said. "A bit of free land that is up for public domain."

"How's that?" I asked.

"Oh, some of the stampeders stepped off five hundred feet straight, some followed the curve of the riverbank. So when the surveyor goes around, he remeasures. And if there is a little land between the two claims, the first man to stake it, gets it.

"But to be realistic," he continued, "I'd say it is best to go work for Ladue's sawmill, make a decent wage, and return home."

"Is that what you are going to do?" I asked.

Sam grinned. "Guess I'm a gambler, Erickson. I guess I'll just keep hanging around Dawson, waiting for a chance to stampede. That's why I came."

He hugged me again and asked if I wanted to join up with him and his two partners. His two partners were sick in their tent, he said.

I said no, I had my kid brother with me now.

Still, it made me feel good that he asked. And he said if he heard of a stampede, he would try to find me. He said we should keep in touch on the bulletin board at the Alaska Commercial Company store, the only way to keep in contact in this town.

The next day I wrote Sam a note and tacked it to the bulletin board, just to see if it would work:

Sam:

I have plenty of citrus extract tablets if your partners need some. Meet me here, early A.M.

Your friend,
J. Erickson

Sam was not there the next morning, but a note was:

J. Erickson:

Thanks. But they are sick of citrus extract tablets.

Sam

P.S. This thing works, don't it?

Tip and I wandered around another day, spending some time storing our supplies in the A.C. Company warehouse. We still slept on our raft, to save money. But we ate in a tent cafeteria so we could stampede at the first whisper.

The next day I saw a note with my name on the bulletin board, folded three times with a nail pounded through the middle. It was so tiny I almost missed it. Quickly I pried out the nail and opened the note:

J. Erickson:

Hear W. Ogilvie is off to adjust claims on the creek hills. You might find something. Partners are better. Now I'm sick.

Sam

I wrote back:

Thanks, Sam. Guess I'm a gambler too.

Your friend,
J. Erickson

And Tip and I were off to the goldfields.

We walked eastward through town, casually, so as not to start a stampede, and found a trail leading up the hill. We followed it through an undergrowth of alder and willow, although the hillside was almost stripped of trees. Tents were perched awkwardly on the muddy slope.

Near the top I whispered, "Do you think anyone is following?"

"Should I turn around?" Tip asked.

"Sure," I whispered. "If I am leading a pack, I want to know."

Tip stooped down as if to check her boots, and peered around.

"Nobody," she said, disgusted.

"Oh, well," I said, wondering why I was disappointed. "That's the way we want it."

We climbed over the crest of the hill and ran down the trail to the edge of the Klondike River, roaring from the east to meet the mighty Yukon around the bend. Across the river from where we stood, the swift waters of Bonanza Creek flowed into the Klondike.

On the steep bank of the Klondike, a cable ferry with a boxlike seat stretched across the river. A sign nailed to a tree stump read: FREE FERRY.

Tip began shaking her head, but I pushed her on fast and jumped on beside her. We pulled ourselves over to the fabulous Bonanza.

For fourteen miles the swift Bonanza Creek twisted down a narrow valley, splashing in and out of man-made sluices, depositing gold. Prospectors in rubber hip boots splashed through the stream, crouched over the sluices, and squatted on the creek banks, whirling gold pans. Gravel dumps and tailings, tents and outhouses dotted the banks and benches.

"At last," I cried, "the golden stream." I jumped

into its icy waters, crunching its gold beneath my boots.

"All the flowers are ruined," Tip said.

I looked at my partner, the Flower Queen.

"We are looking for gold, Tip," I said. "There is nothing more important than gold—flowers, trees, birds. Remember that.

"Now," I said, crawling out of the creek and shaking myself like a husky dog, "we must keep one eye on the hills, looking for Ogilvie, the surveyor. We cannot be watching other men's gold in the valley and miss our only chance on the hills."

I had made up my mind to take any fraction—two inches or two feet. I had not come North to seek my fortune in a sawmill.

It was almost midnight and yet still a dusky twilight when we reached a small camp called Grand Forks, at the junction of Eldorado Creek and Bonanza Creek. The camp was clustered around a two-story hotel.

"Let's stay in the hotel," Tip exclaimed, "in real beds!" She reached into her pocket.

I shook my head. "Save it for tomorrow."

We stayed in a tent behind the hotel that offered bacon, beans, and a cot for fifty cents.

It did not take long for me to find out that the other men in the tent were there for the same reason we were—to grab a fraction. And I resolved that I would grab one first.

Early the next morning they rose quietly and left quickly. Tip and I followed. Soon we were all following an Englishman in a khaki uniform, carrying surveying instruments, who must have dropped from the sky.

"He stayed in the hotel," Tip said.

On Gold Hill, across the Bonanza and above the camp, Ogilvie found a fraction, six feet wide, between two claims.

"Six feet ain't wide enough," one man exclaimed, throwing his hat to the ground.

"It's better than six inches," another said.

"Could be six feet of solid gold."

"Could be a six-foot blank."

The men paced back and forth in front of the fraction, wanting it, but not wanting to make fools of themselves.

"If we stake this, by law we can't stake again in this territory."

"Maybe there will be a twelve-foot fraction on the next hill."

"Well, this is not big enough for a shaft."

"Perhaps a shaft, but you couldn't tunnel. You'd be on another man's claim."

While they talked, I walked over to a tent nearby, picked up two pieces of wood, and started whittling the ends with my pocketknife. I scratched our names on each piece: Erickson and Trattner. Then I walked back to the fraction and pounded down the stakes.

When they heard the pounding, the men became agitated and pounced on me.

"Hey, what do you think you're doing?" one shouted.

Another man reached down and yanked out my stake. "This ain't kid stuff," he said, tossing it over his shoulder.

Ogilvie had been talking to the owners of the adjoining claims. He now walked over. "Do you know the penalty for pulling out a man's stake?" he roared. "And in front of the surveyor, too?"

The man laughed. "That ain't no man's stake. He ain't no eighteen years old."

The other men chuckled.

The surveyor looked at me. "How old are you, young man?"

I thought faster than I had ever thought before. "My partner and I together are twenty-eight years old. It's a partnership claim," I said. "Read the stakes."

All heads turned to Ogilvie.

He walked over to my first stake and read it aloud, "Erickson and Trattner." Then he picked up a rock and hammered it back into the ground.

"Got fifteen dollars to register your claim?" he asked.

"You bet," Tip said, reaching into her pocket.

"You bet," I echoed.

Ogilvie picked up his equipment and started to move on. "If anyone tampers with this claim—Erickson and Trattner," he said, "he will get a 'blue ticket' out of the territory."

He called back to Tip and me. "If you have any trouble registering in Dawson, tell Old Fawcett that Old Ogilvie will be in soon."

We took off running back down the Bonanza. I don't remember my feet touching the ground. I just remember Tip singing at my side like a wound-up mechanical bird:

And when the verse am through,
In the chorus all join in,
There'll be a hot time in the old town tonight!

"Stop singing, Tip," I shouted. "Stop singing and run. The sooner we get there, the sooner we'll be millionaires!"

CHAPTER 10

CRAZY CARIBOU CLYDE

Prospecting for gold on a six-foot string of hillside had its limitations. In fact, burrowing into a hill was not what any stampeder had in mind when he rushed to the Klondike with his pick, shovel, and gold pan.

As Snorin' Sam had said, the golden hills had been a late discovery, in March 1898. As two cheechakos were dragging firewood down the slopes, they saw gold shining in the furrows behind. They tried to keep it a secret, but as soon as they registered their claim, there was another stampede.

There was gold in the hills, all right, but it could not be scooped up in pans as in the streams below. Shafts had to be dug to bedrock in search of the elusive White Channel, which many years earlier had been the original streambed amassing the gold.

That White Channel meandered through the hills, and Tip and I were hoping it meandered down through our narrow claim.

"It has to cross our land at some point," I said firmly, as if saying it would make it so.

Tip sat in front of me, scooping for gold with her boot.

Our two neighbors on the right, Tall Joe and Short Joe, scowled at us as they worked their gravel dump. They had dug one shaft before the spring thaw, and now they were cleaning up with a crude wooden "rocker."

They worked night and day to get rich fast—and also, I suppose, to keep an eye on us.

Our neighbor on the left was crazy. And hairy. His thick gray hair pushed out from under a floppy felt hat, it sprouted out into long whiskers, and it curled around the neck of his red flannel underwear. His baggy trousers were held up with an old frayed rope.

Around Grand Forks he was called Crazy Caribou. It was from his claim that our fraction had been taken, and we decided it was best to stay out of his way.

"I don't like the way he keeps peering at us," Tip said, "around the corners of that cabin he is building."

"He's crazy."

"We're crazy too," Tip said, "sitting single file on this mountain."

"Yes, and we are going to be crazy rich," I said, pulling up a chunk of moss, "if that White Channel just crosses our fraction somewhere."

I tried to think of a plan, but the only thing I could think of was how much I wanted a moose steak at the Grand Forks Hotel.

"It comes with free applesauce," Tip said. "Let's go."

We had heard that the hotel owner, Belinda Mulroney, served free applesauce. It prevented scurvy. And it kept the miners coming in.

We were enjoying our moose steaks and applesauce when our two neighbors on the right sauntered in. They slumped against the bar, looking tired and bored. When they saw us, they brightened.

"Well, if it ain't the six-foot kids," Tall Joe shouted.

Everyone looked at us.

"What I want to know," Short Joe said, grinning, "is this. Are they going to build a six-foot cabin, or live in an outhouse?"

Tall Joe drew an outhouse in the air, walked in, and sat down. Short Joe squeezed in behind.

The miners roared with laughter. And chewed savagely.

"Ignore them," I said to Tip.

The two Joes continued to bullyrag, just to see how long the other men would laugh. And the men kept laughing and slapping their knees.

We ignored them, because that's what you do unless you are riding the horse. I had learned that from the cowboys in Rock Springs.

We concentrated on our expensive moose steaks. I did not know about Tip's, but mine began to taste like fried cardboard. I nearly choked on it.

Short Joe was back at the bar, leading a chant. "The outhouse kids, the outhouse kids!" Soon other miners joined in. They leaned back in their chairs, rocking and chanting. It was a nightmare.

At the far end of the room, under a staircase, a miner stood up. He shuffled across the sawdust floor, carrying his bowl of applesauce. It was our crazy neighbor on the left.

I nudged Tip. "Time to head out."

But before we had a chance to move, that crazy man stepped up to the bar and dumped his bowl of applesauce over Short Joe's head.

Silence filled the room.

"Come on, boys," he said, motioning to us. "Let's go."

We grabbed our moose steaks with our napkins and followed the ragged old man out the door.

After that we were called Crazy Caribou's kids. We did not mind at all.

We moved into the unfinished cabin with Crazy Caribou Clyde Hartwell. He was a music-store clerk from Seattle, Washington. He had been one of the first to reach the Yukon the summer of 1897, before the food requirement. And he had nearly starved that first winter. Scurvy had sapped his strength and taken his teeth. Also his partner. He was thirty-nine years old, but he looked ninety-nine to me.

Caribou needed a partner for shaft mining, and he needed supplies. Tip and I needed a cabin for winter and definitely a larger claim.

We agreed to pool all we had, bring up the gold, and the following summer head for the Outside, dragging our gold with us.

"There is one thing I want to do as soon as I get Outside," I said.

"What's that?" Caribou asked.

"After I arrive in San Francisco," I said, "I would like to toss a few nuggets from a window of the Palace Hotel."

"We'll throw nuggets out of every hotel in the city," Caribou said. I think he was grinning under all his bushy whiskers.

"How can we trust him?" Tip whispered when he was up the hill chopping firewood. "We may slave all winter in his mine shafts while he eats our food. And one morning next spring we may wake up and find him gone with all the gold."

"I am getting good at judging character," I said, though I had to admit the applesauce dump had influenced me. "It comes with experience. I think he is a little peculiar, but all right."

But we had no other choice.

Caribou cooked a stew for us that first night, from our supplies: tinned corn beef with dehydrated carrots, potatoes, and onions. Dumplings on top. And hot chocolate. It was better than anything Tip and I had mixed together.

He served us first. Then, hesitantly, he pulled out a small screen, placed it over a bowl, and began straining his vegetables.

"I have a problem," he mumbled. "No teeth. On account of the scurvy."

I glanced at Tip, and she nodded.

"We have a problem too." I cleared my throat for courage. "One of us is a girl."

Caribou's hairy jaws dropped, and his hand stopped in midair. He looked at me. Then at Tip. Then back at me.

"Rattling roosters!" he said. "So is Belinda Mulroney." He continued straining the vegetables.

I wasn't so sure he was not crazy, after all.

Then Tip nodded toward me. "When *her* hair

grows out," Tip said slowly, "*she* will wear it pompadour."

I looked at Clyde Hartwell and then at Tzipporah Timothy Trattner. And I began to wonder if the North made everyone a little crazy, each in his own way. Perhaps even me.

CHAPTER 11

ON GOLD HILL

We finished the cabin in late August, just before the first snows of winter. It stood in a cluster of low birch trees near the top of Gold Hill, facing east. From our door we had a fine view of the valley below: Bonanza and Eldorado Creeks, Grand Forks, and the rolling hills beyond.

The cabin was small, not much bigger than our raft, because Caribou had hoped for only one partner, not two. And he had not expected a little queen who deserved a separate room with twenty mattresses on her bed.

For the present, the queen had the top bunk on the north wall with a flowered curtain that pulled across. I had the bottom bunk, and Caribou built his along the west wall.

On the south wall was a pickle-bottle window—three rows of green jars, chinked together with moss and mud. This gave us pleasant light, but a distorted view of the world outside.

In the center of the cabin stood our Yukon stove. Hanging above it from the rafters was our tin of sourdough starter, still bubbling. We had rigged up a pulley to lower or raise it, according to the temperature of the stove.

We built a small table and two benches from birch logs, which we placed next to the window.

After that, there was not much room left for anything else except for firewood and our supplies. We stacked them wherever there was an empty spot.

It had been a long time since I had climbed into bed with a real roof over my head. And this cabin had a real roof. I had hoisted the spruce logs up there myself, and I had hauled moss and sod and gravel up a ladder to layer on top.

"Start snowing, start blowing, start freezing," I said, as I curled up on my mattress stuffed with wild hay. "I am ready!"

So it started. In September.

One morning the water in our drinking pail had turned to ice. Caribou hopped around in his red flannels, waving the tin ladle.

"Rattling roosters. Let's go after the gold!"

"So where do we dig?" I asked when we went outside. I stood on the frozen ground with my arms full of wood. It did not make sense to me— waiting for the ground to freeze, then building a fire to thaw it.

Even the ground is crazy up North. It stays frozen all year long except for the top foot or two, which thaws during the summer. Shafts dug in the summer fill up with mud faster than a man can dig. Therefore, shafts are dug in the winter.

"That's as good a place as any," Caribou said, rubbing his whiskers. "Right where you're standing."

I lowered my arms, and the blocks of wood rolled to the ground. And that was where we started our first shaft.

We stacked the wood in an area about four feet wide and started the fire. After it burned down, we scraped the ashes away. Then we picked and shoveled, throwing the dirt into a dump, which immediately froze again.

For one year I had toiled for treasure that had been only a dream at the end of the Yukon River. Now the treasure lay under my feet, perhaps ten feet, perhaps twenty. Nothing would stop me from finding it now. Like a mighty Viking, I swung my heavy pick into the scorched black earth.

That was what I did every day—burn, scrape,

and dig. Except for Sundays, when we rested.

And drank spruce-needle tea. Caribou made us drink a cup every Sunday to prevent scurvy. He went to great trouble to get fresh spruce, and he was always successful, pulling a sprig from his pocket or from under his cap.

I told him I had two pounds of citrus extract tablets expressly for the prevention of scurvy. He nibbled a tablet and said it was not potent enough to prevent a head cold.

He always remembered the tea on Sunday, because it was a different day. Besides drinking the tea, we slept late, read the Bible, and told jokes.

I was not too good with the jokes, since my best one—Pa's dental story—I could not tell to Caribou. But after some of those Bible stories, the jokes were an absolute necessity.

Our daily routine was more practical: burn, scrape, dig. Feed the stove. Cook the beans. Crawl into bed.

Often on Saturday nights we walked down to Belinda Mulroney's hotel for supper. Tip and I had moose steaks and applesauce. Caribou had moose stew and applesauce.

Caribou always carried a tin of food from our supplies in his pocket. The miners eagerly exchanged a pinch of gold dust for a pound of sugar or a tin of condensed milk. And when he took a cup of our sourdough starter, they paid with gold nuggets.

And we enjoyed the moose and applesauce.

Belinda made a big fuss over the queen, after she found out she was a girl. She often sent things home with her, like sheet music, bottles of French perfume, and oilcloth for the table.

Once she gave Tip one of her old hats—a large purple and gold pansy with honey bees swarming above, attached by long delicate wires. We hung it from the rafters above the table like a chandelier.

The next morning we would sleep late and begin our Sunday routine: drink the tea, read the Bible, and tell jokes. Later on, we added guitar music.

There were days that were too cold to work in the shaft, almost too cold to breathe. Then we cleaned the cabin and cooked extra pots of beans. We put the beans outside in our icebox—two wooden crates nailed to a birch tree. On regular days we could chop off a chunk of beans and heat them quickly in a frying pan. We also had a good supply of frozen blueberries that we had picked during the fall.

It was on one of these cold days that Tip found the guitar.

"Whose guitar?" she exclaimed, pulling it out from under Caribou's bunk.

"Who's snooping?" Caribou shouted. He was watching the beans boil.

"I wouldn't call it snooping in a little house like this," Tip said. "It was just there."

"Can you play it?" I asked.

"No," Caribou said sharply. "Put it back."

"But if you packed it over Chilkoot Pass, and across the lakes, and down the Yukon River," Tip said, "you must know how to play it."

"Well, I don't," he said.

As Tip bent down to replace the guitar, she stroked a loud chord across the strings. "Out of tune," she said. She fidgeted with the strings, then strummed again.

"Let me try," I said. I plucked at the strings and made even worse sounds.

It was more than a musician could stand.

"Give it to me," Caribou said. He grabbed the guitar and cradled it like a baby. He played "Yankee Doodle," fast, to make us laugh.

Then he pulled a bench over near the stove, sat down, and sang the most beautiful song I had ever heard:

I dream of Jeanie with the light brown hair,
Borne, like a vapor on the summer air,
I see her tripping where the bright streams play,
Happy as the daisies that dance on her way.

Caribou was looking through the pickle-bottle window, far away. Tears began rolling down his cheeks into his matted whiskers.

"Who's Jeanie?" Tip asked in a forlorn voice.

"Don't know," he said. He pulled out a red handkerchief from his pocket and blew his nose.

I did not know a Jeanie either. There was a calendar picture on our south wall of a beautiful girl with pink roses tumbling down her light brown hair. Coca-cola was written under her picture. I thought maybe she was Jeanie.

After we had dug several feet into the ground, we could no longer throw out the dirt. It was necessary to build a windlass.

We shored up the sides of the shaft with timber, built a platform on the surface, and constructed a hand winch for pulling a bucket up and down.

The hillsides were dotted with windlasses, creaking like old bones. In the evenings they gave off a pink glow from the fires left to burn out during the night.

Every few days we took a sample of dirt from our shaft into the cabin and washed it in our gold pan, hoping to find promise of "pay dirt" below.

"Smile on us, Lady Luck," Caribou always said as he whirled the pan. He looked up in the general direction of the pansy hat. "Smile on us!"

"She did not smile," Tip said, night after night.

Through the dark Northern days I toiled in

the depths of the earth. My arms ached, my back ached, and my hands were blistered. But I told myself each day that if there would just be a thin layer of gold waiting at bedrock, it would be worth all the misery.

Tip and I were at the surface dumping dirt when Caribou hit bedrock. We could hear him striking against the hard rock.

We both dropped to our knees and peered down the dark shaft.

"Is it pay dirt?" I shouted.

Caribou did not answer, but we could hear him down there, shoveling and mumbling. In a few minutes he called, "Pull 'er up!"

We raised the bucket and, when it reached the surface, pulled it over to the platform. I frowned at its blackness.

We heard Caribou climbing up the cribbing, and soon he emerged from the shaft, his face smeared with soot and dirt. I knew without asking that there had been no gold waiting at bedrock. We had drawn a "blank."

CHAPTER 12

KLONDIKE WINTER

We did what any other frustrated Klondike miner would do—we started digging another shaft. This time we chose a spot on the south side of the claim, over on our fraction.

Our neighbors, Tall Joe and Short Joe, started a new shaft too, just opposite ours. As they worked they stared at us.

We stared back.

The digging was slow. It snowed so much we had trouble keeping a fire burning. When the snow stopped, it was too cold to stay outside long.

The three of us took turns, two outside digging and one in the cabin cooking. Before long, Tip was spending most of her time inside. She was the best cook. Anyway, that's what Caribou and I told her.

Once she made a cake. She used real eggs that Belinda Mulroney brought from Dawson City. She baked the cake in a frying pan, all four layers, and covered it with Eagle Brand frosting. Then she covered it with shredded coconut. And then frozen blueberries.

It looked like another hat chandelier!

Dawson City had almost everything in the world—like eggs—for a price. Although Tip and I both had a little cash tucked under the mattress, we still lived off our supplies, supplementing them with berries and rabbits. And, occasionally, a Saturday-night splurge at Belinda's hotel.

Belinda Mulroney had sled dogs—three malamutes, white as snow, except for their black ears, which she kept covered with bonnets. Belinda took her dogs to Dawson City often, bringing back supplies and sometimes letters for the miners around Grand Forks.

Once that winter she brought a letter for Caribou. I knew who it was from right away, because earlier Tip had found a packet of letters the same size and color under his bunk with his guitar.

"Who's Josephine?" Tip had demanded, holding up the packet tied with a string. "Josephine from Seattle?"

"Who's snooping again?" Caribou roared. "Put them back!" He was washing a sample of dirt, looking for color.

"Who is she?" Tip insisted.

"Maybe an old friend, Tipsy," Caribou said. He

whirled the pan so fast that water splashed over the edge.

"If I had an old friend," Tip said, "I would be so happy I would talk about her. Who is she?"

"It's his Jeanie," I said sharply. "His wife. Now, that's enough."

I envied the Klondike kings that winter as they dashed up and down the frozen creeks with their dog teams. They came from Dawson City, swaggering into Belinda's hotel, laughing and swinging small bags filled with gold.

When a Klondike king threw down a poke of gold at the bar, it meant free drinks and entertainment for everyone who could squeeze inside.

In Dawson City the saloonkeeper rang a bell and all the men on the street rushed in. They grabbed a drink and a pretty girl, and whirled around the sawdust floor. All compliments of the Klondike king.

In Grand Forks the men danced by themselves or with calendar girls, which they snatched right off the walls.

I wanted to be a Klondike king. I had worked as hard as any of them had. Why had I drawn a blank?

"Life is not fair," Caribou said, as we trudged through deep snow down to the hotel. "We do our best with it." He sounded like my pa.

I thought of Pa often, those long winter nights when the northern lights crackled and flashed. The first time I saw them flashing through our window, I thought the mountain was on fire. I jumped from my bunk and ran to the door, shouting for Caribou.

Outside, lights flashed across the sky, yellow and red, like someone waving a torch. The flames hissed in the bitter cold night.

"It's the aurora borealis," Caribou said.

"The what?"

"The northern lights," he explained. "The Eskimos say the lights are torches, carried by spirits to guide travelers on their journey to heaven."

"It's a nice way to go," I said.

During that long, bitter-cold winter, I liked to think that Pa was one of those spirits with a torch, and that he waved it over our cabin, just for me.

I felt he was sending a message to me, if only my earthbound senses could figure it out. I told that to no one, however. Except Tip, because she told me about her betrayed mother.

"My mother was not a lady of the evening," she announced one night, leaning over the edge of her top bunk. The wind screeching around the cabin kept us both awake, although Caribou slept soundly.

"Is this a song?" I asked.

"Of course it isn't a song. Why would you think—"

"No reason," I said quickly.

"My mother was a professional actress," Tip said. "When she was young, she was always hanging around the theater, back in Chicago, where she lived. Her parents wanted her to be a nurse or a teacher, anything but an actress. They were afraid she would marry a poor actor who would run out on her.

"Once a traveling troupe offered her a dramatic part. She wrote her parents a note, and left. She wrote letters to her parents many times, but they did not answer.

"Well, she married one of the actors in the juggling act," Tip continued. "And they had me. Then he left. Starving actors do that, you know."

I nodded. "Just like her parents said."

"Later my mother heard he died. She cried a lot over him. I did too. I even cry over him now sometimes," Tip said softly, "and I never even knew him."

"That's all right," I said. "He was your pa."

"My mother became a dance-hall girl to make more money, to support me. I cry over her sometimes too."

"I know that. I talk right out loud to my pa."

"I know that, too."

"You have your grandmother Tzipporah somewhere Outside," I said.

"I have been thinking about her," Tip said. "I could look her up and see if she is still angry."

"I don't think either one of your grandparents will be angry," I said.

"Do you have grandparents to look up when you go Outside?"

"Sure," I lied. "Lots of them. But once I have the gold, I won't need to look up anybody."

One night in November, the Perry Davis Painkiller outside our door froze. Caribou and I had rigged up a thermometer—five small pickle bottles of liquid that froze at different temperatures. We secured these in a rack and nailed it to the cabin. The liquids froze in this order:

Quicksilver:	-40 °F
Kerosene:	-50 °F
Jamaica Ginger Extract:	-60 °F
Perry Davis Painkiller:	-70 °F
Hudson Bay Rum:	-80 °F

"The Perry Davis froze," Caribou muttered as he shuffled back to bed in his red flannels. "Don't get out of bed."

"Wasn't just Davis," I squeaked, shrinking down in my covers. My breath was white on the air.

Caribou grabbed a fur robe from a bench and piled it on top of Tip. "The Arctic is no place for a little queen," he mumbled.

Then he pulled a blanket from his bunk and spread it over me.

"Keep your blanket," I said. "I don't need it."

"I'm too hot," he said, pulling his trousers on over his red flannels. He was acting a lot like my pa.

The next morning I woke up to the noise of sawing wood. Then I discovered I was making the noise. With each difficult breath, a pain shot through my chest.

Tip leaned over the edge of her bunk. "What's the matter?" she asked.

"My—my lungs are frozen," I gasped.

She crawled down and hopped over the cold floor to Caribou's bunk. "The tea—the tea did not work," she cried, shaking him. "James has scurvy!"

Caribou bolted from his bed and leaned over me. "Light the candle fast, Tip," he said.

It was not scurvy. It was pneumonia.

For days Caribou sat by my bedside, wrapped in a fur robe, blaming himself. He said he never should have let me work like a man in a dark, damp mine. After all, I was still a growing boy. He moaned and groaned until I thought he was sick too.

He rubbed my back with St. Jacob's Oil and ladled out big doses of Perry Davis Painkiller.

Three times a day he applied his master treatment, a mustard plaster.

For this he stirred up a yellow concoction and spread it on a square of old flannel underwear. "This is going to hurt me more than you," he said each time, and he'd slap it on my bare chest.

"It's burning!" I yelled the first time. "You must have the wrong recipe."

"No," he said. He rubbed his hand through his hair, streaking it yellow. "A heaping tablespoon of mustard to a heaping cup of flour. And boiling water. No recipe to it."

It is strange what you remember when you think you are dying. I remembered the last note from Snorin' Sam when he told me about the fraction. He had also said he was sick. I was sorry I had not cared enough to check on him. I wanted to now, and I hoped it was not too late.

Tip wrote the note for me:

Sam from the Guardian:

Where are you? Hope you got better. I still have the citrus extract tablets. Also have a good fraction on Gold Hill, thanks to you.

Your friend,
James Erickson

Also I remembered a promise I had made to Tip about her mother's fur coat. I had said I would get it for her as soon as we reached Dawson City.

"Don't worry about it now," Tip said. "On our next trip to Dawson, I will look up the Flower Girls and get it back."

Caribou said what we all needed was a spree in Dawson City. "But until we strike it rich," he said, "how about a rabbit hunt? That is, as soon as James gets better."

I agreed, and he slapped on another mustard plaster.

As soon as I recovered, Tip became sick. She was not really sick with anything, but she lay in her bunk and looked at the rafters all day long. Caribou called it "cabin fever" and took her down to Grand Forks to stay with Belinda Mulroney for a few days.

"We don't want any cabin fever in this cabin," Caribou said. "There just isn't room."

Tip seemed happy when she came back. She had new jokes to tell us, and she had learned a new song, which she sang night and day. It livened up the cabin:

Casey would waltz with a strawberry blonde,
And the band played on.
He'd glide 'cross the floor with the girl he
adored,
And the band played on.

But his brain was so loaded it nearly exploded,
The poor girl would shake with alarm.
He'd ne'er leave the girl with the strawberry
curls,
And the band played on.

The sun disappeared for two months during December and January, but Christmas arrived just the same. Early in December, during a clear spell, Caribou and I went out looking for a Christmas tree. We found a fine blue spruce at the top of Gold Hill, which we cut down and slid over the crusted snow to our cabin.

We could barely squeeze it through the door, and once inside it seemed to fill the entire cabin. We moved the table and the pansy hat and stood the tree in front of the window.

Tip unraveled a red sweater that was too small for her, and night after night we tied yarn bows on the ends of the branches. On the very top we placed a shining silver star cut from a Lowney's Cocoa can.

For two months the tree filled our cabin with beauty and, also, with the scent of spruce-needle tea.

After Christmas, Belinda asked if Tip would like to go to Dawson City with her for a few days. She was building a new hotel on Front Street, and she went there often.

Of course Tip wanted to go. I was glad because she took my note to Sam and promised to post it on the A.C. Company bulletin board.

Caribou and I watched the two of them pull away from Grand Forks in Belinda's dog sled, her three malamutes howling like wolves and swinging their tails above their backs. My dog team, I vowed, would never wear baby bonnets.

Tip turned and waved. We waved.

We watched them racing down the frozen Bonanza Creek until they disappeared from view.

Caribou turned to me. "Now that the womenfolk are gone," he asked, "what should we men do?"

It did not take us long to decide. We went on a rabbit hunt.

CHAPTER 13

FOR LOVE OF TIP

One day in January, Tip announced that she was going to sing and dance Saturday nights at the Grand Forks Hotel for pay. She said she was tired of eating beans and dressing like a boy. And— she danced around the cabin, holding a pretend mirror—her hair was now long enough to wear pompadour.

"Not on your pretty little life!" Caribou shouted. He slammed the frying pan down on the stove.

"What does that mean?" Tip demanded.

"That means *no*," I said.

"He is not my dad," Tip said, bursting into tears. She fled to her top bunk and pulled the curtain.

It was cabin fever again.

Caribou said he understood that Tip needed to be around a woman for a few days. "Someone who wears dresses and bakes layer cakes—"

"And crochets bonnets for her dogs," I added.

We all knew Belinda Mulroney was the only woman around.

"As for the beans"—Caribou rubbed his whiskers—"I am sick of beans, too. I will go on a moose hunt for you, Tipsy, though I may come home with a rabbit. And when spring comes—in May—we will go dress shopping in Dawson City.

"But," he continued, "no singing and dancing for pay. That is not for a little queen."

After a long silence Tip parted the curtain. She nodded her head.

Caribou smiled. "So we will meet at Belinda's on Saturday night and come home together," he said.

By Saturday, Caribou and I were tired of digging all day in the mine and cooking for ourselves. So we stayed in the cabin and cleaned up. We washed our clothes in a small wooden tub and hung them on a line overhead. We each took a bath standing up in the tub, shivering. Caribou trimmed his beard and then he cut my hair.

Feeling great, we raced down the snow-crusted hill to the hotel.

"Where's Tipsy?" Caribou called, rushing through the hotel door.

Belinda was behind the bar, polishing glasses, and smiling. She was wearing a fashionable outfit, a white shirtwaist and a long dark skirt. Her hair was in a high pompadour. Still, she did not look like the girls on her hotel calendars.

"I let her go into Dawson to sing—with Hughie," she said.

"You what?" Caribou slammed his fist on the bar. "You let her what?"

"Like I said"—Belinda shrugged—"I let her go to Dawson with Hughie, the piano player. She's a talented kid. She has friends there. Her mother's singing group. She'll be just fine, so calm down, Daddy."

As she turned to set the glasses on a shelf behind her, Caribou reached over and grabbed one of her long puffed sleeves. The glasses dropped from her hands.

A dreadful silence followed, not unlike another one I remembered in that room.

"Harness your sled dogs, Belinda," Caribou said.

"Fast," I added. "And without the bonnets."

No one borrowed Belinda Mulroney's malamutes, she informed us.

"We are taking, not borrowing," Caribou said. And we rushed back outside.

I dived into a pile of fur robes in the sled, and Caribou ran along behind on the packed snow. When the dogs really started running, he jumped on the back runners.

"Mush on!" we shouted. "Mush on!"

Those dogs ran, all right, their tongues hanging out, their tails waving. They slowed down at times, but they did not stop until we reached Dawson City, three hours later.

Front Street looked deserted, except for a few dog teams tied to hitching posts and a Mountie on patrol. Everyone was inside the saloons, keeping warm.

We searched them all—the Pioneer, the Dominion, the Opera House, the Aurora Saloon. And half a dozen others. Their grand facades all looked the same: two-storied wooden fronts with ornate balconies, and large bay windows inscribed with their names.

They all looked the same inside, too, except for the stuffed moose heads in the Pioneer and the nude murals in the Flora Dora.

"This is no place for a little queen," Caribou said, wincing at the murals.

Inside each saloon we headed straight for the dance hall, where miners lined up at one dollar a dance around the sawdust floor. Almost as soon as a pretty girl was in a man's arms, a caller would shout, "Belly up to the bar, now."

As the miner drank, the girl collected her commission from the bartender—a small ivory disk that she tucked into her stockings. Then with a smile, and lumpy legs, she reached out for her next partner.

We found Tip in the Monte Carlo, whirling in

the arms of a squatty, red-bearded miner. A white feather from her hair rested on his shoulder.

Caribou began snorting like an enraged bull and his cheeks turned flame red.

"I'll get her," I whispered, grabbing his arm. "You are too mad."

I pushed through the dancers and tapped her shoulder. "Come on, Tip. Let's get out of here."

She looked up, startled.

"Your grandmother is furious with you," I added.

The miner gave me a shove. "Who do you think you are?" he snarled.

Caribou, charging in, shouted, "I'm her pa!"

"So am I," I shouted. "Out of the way."

It happened so fast that I could not remember five minutes later exactly how we'd done it. Caribou did the heavy pushing, though, and I ran out the front door with Tip. We ducked around the corner of the saloon, and as soon as Caribou came charging past, we grabbed him.

Tip was shivering in her scanty silk dress, even though I had thrown my coat over her shoulders.

"Can you get your clothes," Caribou asked, "through the back entrance?"

She nodded, and we followed her around to the back. Rushing up the stairway, we collided with a dance-hall girl, wrapped in a hooded white fur coat. Only her pale oval face peered out.

"Pansy," Tip exclaimed. "My mother's furs."

Pansy jerked away from her. "I'm in a hurry," she said.

Caribou held out his arms and blocked the stairway. "Whose coat is it?"

"Step aside," Pansy said, and she hit Caribou with a fur muff.

"Just a minute," he said. "Whose coat?"

"It's my mother's," Tip said. "My mother's white fox fur. And the muff. She told me to be sure and keep them."

"You can't prove a thing, you little snip," Pansy scoffed.

"Her name is embroidered in the lining," Tip said.

"Mind if I check?" I asked. I pulled the coat from Pansy's shoulders.

"I'll call the Mounties," she said.

Even in the dim light from a frosted window, we could read the embroidered name: NELL T. TRATTNER.

"I'm going to call the Mounties," Pansy said, grabbing the coat. She was shivering with cold, and I could hear her teeth chattering, or maybe it was the ivory in her stockings.

"Go ahead," I said. "And they will give you a blue ticket out of the territory. For theft."

Realizing she was cornered, Pansy became play-ful. "Is that really you, Jamie?" she asked sweetly. "Young Jamie, all grown up?"

She sidled up close to me, pouting. "Now, you wouldn't take a coat off a poor girl's back, would you?"

"You could say that." I was too cold to argue. I grabbed the fur coat with one hand, the muff with the other. "You could say that."

That night we dashed home to our cabin on Gold Hill—Tip and me in the sled, Caribou standing behind, shouting at the dogs. They needed no driving, however. They knew they were going home too.

The snow snapped beneath our sled and the harness bells jingled merrily. Overhead the stars glowed with a warmth I had not felt before.

Suddenly the northern lights flashed across the sky in brilliant colors, crackling like fireworks. That was Pa, all right, racing around up there with his torches, applauding.

"I have been thinking," Caribou called from behind. "Tipsy, how would you like to sing Saturday nights at Belinda's hotel with this old man on gui-tar? No dancing, just singing?"

"I'd like that," Tip exclaimed, jumping up to hug

Caribou. "And also," she said, as the sled careened, "thank you both for rescuing me. I did not like the dancing."

This was the closest to a family I had ever come, since Pa and me. It felt too good to lose. Now I had something to say, and I just blurted it out.

"After this gold rush is over, should we stay together? The three of us—and Josephine?"

"Sounds good to me," Caribou said. I could tell by his voice that he was smiling.

"Me too," Tip said. She reached up and kissed Caribou on his cheek, and then she threw both her arms around me. A frozen feather poked me in the chin.

I was glad for the dark night and all the furs. "Me too," I said.

CHAPTER 14

GOLD FEVER

Long before spring cleanup, before the melting snow rushed down the hillside into our sluice box, we knew we had struck it rich. Our gravel dumps glittered with color. And every time we washed a sample, the pan yielded golden nuggets the size of navy beans. All our empty food tins were now filled with gold.

"I think we are millionaires," Caribou announced one night, bouncing the wet gold pan on his knee. A small mound of shining gold lay in the curve of the pan.

"I've been thinking the same thing," I said.

We grinned at each other.

"Thank you, Lady Luck," Tip shouted. She reached up and whirled the pansy hat over the table. Then she ran over to her bunk and pulled down the white fur coat. She danced around the room in it, swinging the muff like a feather boa.

"After we go on a spree," she asked, "then what?"

No one answered. I was far away with my own thoughts of Wyoming and horses and gold-studded saddles. And thick beefsteak.

Caribou was talking to a faded picture of his Josephine. "I am wealthy," he whispered. "But I'm a toothless old man." He covered his face with his large rough hands. And moaned.

Tip put her arms around him, patting his shoulder. "She will love you just the same, Caribou. Don't fret about it."

She plopped down on his lap like a playful pup. "Have you ever heard of false teeth, Caribou? Lots of rich old men have them. They click a little, but—"

Caribou smiled, a bit sadly. "You are right, my Tipsy. Who cares about a little clicking?"

For no particular reason except that I was almost a millionaire, I grabbed the muff from Tip. She grabbed it back. We jostled back and forth with it, until we heard it rip.

"Now look what you're done," she cried. "You have torn it."

I felt sorry, and I reached inside to see what damage I had caused. My hand slid inside the torn lining and touched something peculiar—an envelope. I drew it out quickly. It was addressed to Tzipporah Trattner.

"What is it?" Tip asked.

"I think this is the reason your mother told you to keep her furs," I said. "Open it."

She did not open the envelope immediately. She stared at it and turned it over and over, like Caribou had done with Josephine's picture. Then she slowly broke the seal.

Inside was a packet of one-hundred-dollar bills. And a smaller envelope addressed to Mr. and Mrs. Joseph Timothy in Chicago, Illinois.

"Who are these people?" Tip asked, timidly.

"Your grandparents, I would think," Caribou said.

"Your grandmother Tzipporah," I added.

Tip stood quietly, turning the envelope over and over in her hands. Her eyes filled with tears. Then she clutched the envelope to her heart and, dragging her white furs, climbed up into her bunk. And pulled the curtain.

Perhaps it was then I got the gold fever again. Perhaps it was because Tip had her grandparents and Caribou had his Josephine. And I had only bags of gold. I did not know the reason.

Spring arrived almost without my noticing. One day it was snowing; the next day it was raining. When the mountain began to melt, Caribou and

I deserted our mine shaft and started building a sluice—a long open box with riffles nailed across the bottom.

We dug a ditch, cut a dam into the mountainside, and channeled the rushing water through our sluice box. Day after day we shoveled our gravel dumps into the sluice, and day after day we scooped out the gold.

In late spring, after the runoff, Caribou and I built a rocker to conserve water. It was a small wooden box set on rockers, with a hopper on top and two riffles across the bottom. We took turns shoveling gravel into the hopper, pouring water over with a dipper, and rocking the box with a handle. We used the water collected in our dam over and over again.

"Slow down, James, slow down," Tip yelled daily. She worked outside with us now that it was spring.

"Yes, rattling roosters, slow down," Caribou shouted.

Whenever Tip and Caribou went inside to rest, I kept working, shoveling dirt into the hopper, pouring water over, catching the water, pouring it in again. Scooping up gold dust and nuggets.

"Just because the sun is up all day and night, doesn't mean you should be," Tip said.

I did not listen, because I had gold fever.

On Saturday nights when we went down to Belinda's hotel, I met in a back room with several men who had just arrived in the North. They talked about a new gold rush on the sands of Nome, Alaska, just across the Bering Strait from Siberia.

This new El Dorado had no mountains to climb, no boats to build, and no shafts to dig. Gold simply washed up from the ocean and covered the sandy beaches. And it was just a short steamer cruise to the mouth of the Yukon River and around the bay.

I wanted it. I found a partner called Beans who wanted it too.

"After cleanup," I said. "After what I have is safely shipped to San Francisco."

Tip and Caribou tried to talk me out of it. "You have enough gold," Caribou said. "At least a hundred thousand."

But every time I thought what I could do with one hundred thousand dollars, I thought what I could do with more.

"I can throw a hundred nuggets out the window of the Palace Hotel in one day," I said.

"I thought we all wanted to stay together," Tip said. "Caribou and Josephine and you—and me."

"You will go live with your grandparents," I said.

"Maybe they won't want me."

"They will want you, all right," I said, "with a hundred thousand dollars."

Caribou shook his head sadly.

"You can talk yourself blue," I concluded every conversation. "I am going to Nome."

"It isn't the gold he is after," Tip said one day to Caribou, as she scooped water into the rocker. They were beginning to talk as if I were not around. "It's something to do with his blood. It's Viking."

She threw down the dipper and fled to the cabin.

Near the end of May 1899, Caribou said it was time to go to Dawson City to witness the breaking up of the ice on the Yukon River. I thought this ritual unnecessary, until I realized that anyone watching the ice break on the Yukon River had somehow survived a winter in the Northland—the making of a "sourdough."

Still, I did not want to make the trip to Dawson City, fearing that our bags of gold in the cabin might be stolen.

"You will always be called a cheechako if you don't," Caribou said, "and never a real sourdough. Everyone will be there, and anyone who isn't will look suspicious."

"I saw the ice breakup at Lake Bennett," I said.

"And you are still a cheechako," Caribou answered. "Besides, we need to arrange with the Bartlett brothers for a pack train to carry out our gold in a few weeks."

"And we need to book passage on a steamboat Outside," Tip added. "Belinda says they are grand. Just think of it. Going up the Yukon on a boat, all the way to Lake Bennett."

It was true that after this year's breakup, Dawson City would no longer be completely isolated from civilization. Belinda had told us that a railroad had been built from Skagway over the White Pass to Lake Bennett.

And soon, steamboats would be sailing the length of the Yukon waterway, from Lake Bennett to St. Michael, Alaska.

"Remember Soapy Smith in Skagway?" Tip asked. "He is dead now. Shot by Frank Reid, one of the vigilantes. Reid is dead too. Shot by Soapy. Belinda says Skagway is as clean as a whistle now, because all Soapy's con men left on the first boat Outside."

I remembered Soapy Smith. And just in case any of his men had managed to sneak past the Mounties, I suggested we hide our gold before going to Dawson City.

We cut a hole in the cabin floor and stashed our bags of gold there. Then we covered it with a fur robe and pulled the table over it. Just in case!

Early the next morning, Caribou came into the cabin with a grin on his face. "Tall Joe and Short Joe have struck it rich," he said.

"How do you know?" I asked.

"They are nailing their cabin door shut before they go to Dawson." Caribou chuckled. "Now we won't need to."

In Dawson City we stayed at Belinda Mulroney's new Fairview Hotel on Front Street, compliments of Belinda, who was no doubt trying to make up for our last trip to town. She did a fine job of it too.

The Fairview rooms were steam-heated, and electric lights hung from the ceilings, dazzling us. The shiny brass beds had real cotton sheets and goose-down pillows. In the dining room the tables were spread with linen, sterling silver, and bone china.

The first night for supper we ordered everything on the menu we had never heard of before, like mock turtle soup and piccalilli and Bengal chutney. Most of it turned out to be relish for things we had not ordered, but we ate it all and had plenty of room for pineapple sherbet.

All the time, out in the lobby under shimmering

cut-glass chandeliers, a chamber orchestra played Brahms. And when Belinda told us all this had been packed by men and mules over the White Pass and down the Yukon River on scows, we could hardly eat or sleep for the wonder of it all.

We had ourselves a real spree at the Fairview Hotel. In fact, Caribou and I almost missed the ice breaking up, because we were steaming in the Turkish baths. Luckily, Tip came by in her white furs and pounded on the door. And we all made it down to the river in time.

On May 23 the frozen river cracked like a giant jigsaw puzzle. Then all fury broke loose: Ice piled on top of ice; water rushed over the riverbanks and surged up under the boardwalks of Front Street. We all cheered as we moved back from the water.

Out in midstream a bobcat, looking terrified, crouched on a block of ice whirling down the river. Dogs chased it along the riverbank, yelping and howling. I felt glad that I was not that bobcat.

"We are sourdoughs, Tip," I said, grabbing her hand. "Genuine, bona fide, simon-pure Yukon sourdoughs."

"And crazy rich," Tip shouted.

We danced uninhibited on the boardwalks of the flooded street.

Before we left Dawson City, I went over to the

A.C. Company bulletin board, hoping to find a note from my friend Sam. There was a note, curled and faded, with my name on it. I pulled it from the nail:

J. Erickson:

Sam died last fall. Scurvy. He was a good man.

Pete and Mac, his partners

We rode the stagecoach back to Grand Forks, just the three of us. Caribou did most of the talking.

"I have not told you about my first partner," he said quietly, "my partner last year. He was younger than I, just twenty years old. It's his guitar in the cabin. He packed it over Chilkoot Pass."

He paused for a long time, but I knew he had more to tell.

"Then what?" I asked, trying to help him along.

"Well," he said, "we nearly starved that first winter, and we both got scurvy. But he didn't pull through. I did not know about spruce-needle tea then. I did not know about a lot of things."

I nodded.

"You know I am apprehensive about seeing Josephine again," he continued, "with my frostbitten face and no teeth. But that is not the main reason."

"Oh?" Tip asked.

"He was Josephine's kid brother."

Neither Tip nor I knew what to say. But Tip put her arm around him.

I knew he was trying to tell me something. And I had almost changed my mind about leaving them when we were having our spree at the Fairview. But I would join them later in Seattle or San Francisco. Surely we would be no different.

Besides, there was that thing with my blood. I had already survived Skagway, the Chilkoot Trail, the mighty Yukon River, and a Klondike winter. And now that I knew about spruce-needle tea and mustard plasters, I could survive anything. I was indestructible.

· CHAPTER 15 ·

THE TREASURE

It took ten mules from the Bartlett Freighting Company to carry our gold to Dawson City. Alongside rode the Bartlett brothers and two North West Mounted Police. Caribou, Tip, and I each rode a horse, bringing up the rear of the procession. We followed the Ridge Road along the hills, as the Bartlett brothers advised, rather than passing through the creek claims.

We estimated we were taking out about three hundred thousand dollars in gold dust and nuggets, although it was impossible to tell for certain until we had it assayed at the Canadian Bank of Commerce in Dawson City. We planned to sell most of it to the bank at the current rate of sixteen dollars an ounce. We also planned to keep a few bags for tossing around.

We were not alone on the Ridge Road that July day. Nearly everyone was leaving the Klondike valley. Some sold their claims, as we had, to large commercial companies who were coming in with heavy mining equipment. Others walked away from their claims, worthless or valuable, without looking back. They headed home or toward the new El Dorado in Nome.

The great Klondike Gold Rush was ending, as quickly as it had begun, three years almost to the day since George Carmack discovered gold on Bonanza Creek, two years since the *Excelsior* landed in San Francisco and announced it to the world.

I was two years older—sixteen—and five inches taller. And I had found my fortune.

In Dawson City our pack train attracted a considerable amount of attention. In fact, a crowd followed us, like a parade, as we moved along the south side of town down to the bank on Front Street.

Queen Tzipporah rode her black horse in fine style, balancing the pansy hat on top of her head. She had started out wearing her fur coat, which was now draped like bunting over the horse.

Caribou and I looked all right too, in new plaid shirts and polished boots. We would be purchasing bearskin coats just as soon as we had time.

I heard my name called and looked up. The Flower Girls were waving feather boas and throwing kisses from the balcony of the Monte Carlo.

I waved back.

"Another Klondike king," someone called from the crowd.

"Rich and crazy, I hear."

"Who are the young ones?" another asked.

"They belong to the old man. They are called Crazy Caribou's kids."

"I've heard of them before. They struck it rich on Gold Hill. Had a spree at the new Fairview. Ordered champagne for breakfast."

The crowd murmured and drew back as we dismounted. Caribou winked at Tip and me. Then he motioned for the Bartlett brothers to start unloading.

Tip and Caribou stayed at the Fairview Hotel again. I planned to meet my new partner, Beans, at the Regina, where he had been staying for several days.

When I left Tip and Caribou in the lobby of the Fairview, I felt an uncomfortable prick, although I could not explain it. I was simply changing partners. I was moving on. That is what Pa and I had always done.

Beans was waiting for me on the boardwalk outside the Regina. He slapped me smartly on my back, which brought me out of my melancholy.

I liked Beans. He was older, but still out for adventure.

"By the way"—he slapped me on the back again—"there will be three of us in our partnership.

"Three?"

"You don't object, do you?"

"Of course not," I replied quickly. "Any friend of yours—"

"A friend of mine will be coming in from the Outside on one of the steamboats. Any day now. We have worked together for years."

It was all right with me. I was just anxious to strike out for Nome and more gold. That is, after I had spent some time at the tailor's. My pants came almost up to my knees.

Two days later Beans and I went down to the waterfront to watch the *Northern Maid* leave—with Tip and Caribou and my bags of gold. Two days, and Tip hardly recognized me.

It was because of my new corduroy suit, I suppose. And my stiff white shirt and bow tie and tweed cap. And a gold watch fob, big as my thumb, hanging from my watch chain.

"Th-those new clothes," Tip stammered, "they make you look taller than Caribou." She began to cry.

"It isn't the clothes," Caribou said, almost hugging the breath out of me. "He is taller. And he is sixteen."

I did not like this show of emotion in front of my new partner, so I pushed them aboard the steamer, fast. I had never said good-bye to anyone I cared about in my life. Not Ma. Not Pa. Not anyone. So I did not do a bang-up job of it.

"See you later," I said. And I walked briskly away with Beans.

I turned, after a few minutes, and looked for them. They were on the second deck, squeezing through the crowd to the railing.

Soon the steamboat blew its whistle. And slowly it moved from the dock.

I felt another uncomfortable prick, only this time it was more like a hammer pounding. And I knew I could not ignore the message.

But Beans interrupted.

"What luck," he said, slapping my back. "My friend has arrived. Meet your new partner, Erickson."

I turned and held out my hand.

The man's head was lowered, his eyes scrutinizing my gold watch fob. When he raised his head, I looked directly into his small shifty eyes, not unlike those of a con man I had once known.

"Partner," he said.

I did not hear what either one of those men said next. I just heard my pa coming through loud and clear. "Time to move on, son. But not in that direction."

"I just figured that out, Pa," I said aloud. "Just did."

I almost lost my treasure that day in Dawson City, and not my bags of gold on the freight deck of the *Northern Maid*. My treasure was up on the second deck—a gray-haired man and a skinny girl in white fur.

I ran down to the river, frantically waving my arms. "Stop, stop the boat!"

The steamer was in midchannel, its orange paddle wheel splashing water.

"Stop," I yelled. "Stop!"

Caribou and Tip were leaning over the railing, gesturing hopelessly. Then Caribou grabbed the leather poke hanging from his belt and ran up the narrow stairs to the pilothouse.

I was a crazy fool, yelling and waving at the steamboat. But slowly it turned and eased itself back to shore. It puffed black smoke and blew its shrill whistle—and dropped its gangplank. And I ran aboard.

Passengers crowded around me, asking questions. "What happened, young man? What happened?"

I did not say. I was too breathless.

Finally, when the crowd fell away and the three of us were alone, I said, "Thanks. Thanks for stopping the boat."

"Took half his poke," Tip said. She was fanning herself with her muff.

We leaned against the railing, watching the figures on the waterfront become smaller and smaller, watching Dawson City, the City of Gold in a moose swamp, fade into a mist.

"I never have been able to tell the cons from the regulars—right off," I said.

"Not right off," Tip said.

"Well, now what?" Caribou was grinning, unable to hide his pleasure.

What next? I hardly knew myself, since I had not planned to go in this direction. I remembered the faded green boardinghouse on Rincon Hill, floating in the fog. The attic room that Pa and I had called home. Mrs. Maxwell and her weary boarders. Almo at the livery.

I remembered my faithful horse, Rexy, trotting up and down the cobblestone hills. The old miner with his heavy suitcases.

And remembering, I smiled.

"To the Palace Hotel, partners," I shouted. I put my arms around both of them. "To toss a few gold nuggets from the top-floor windows."